"Lydia!"

She whipped around to find where Wesley had called from. A closed door on the far side of the room. "I'm coming!"

"I told you to get off the boat. Get off now! There's a bomb!"

A bomb?

She could barely hear him through the door, but knew she'd heard him correctly.

A sudden bang echoed in her head and trembled under her feet. The explosion blew the door out, sending her flying back into the far wall at a cataclysmic force.

Dazed and confused, she sat in a hunch against the wall and tried to form a complete thought. She told her body to move—to get to Wesley, who had been in that room. He could be hurt. He may need help. She forced her eyes to open and felt heat dry the surface of her eyes before her brain computed what caused it.

Fire.

"Lydia!"

She heard him call. But she couldn't move.

Books by Katy Lee

Love Inspired Suspense

Warning Signs
Grave Danger

KATY LEE

is an inspirational romantic suspense author writing higher-purpose stories in high-speed worlds. She dedicates her life to sharing tales of love, from the greatest love story ever told to those sweet romantic stories of falling in love. She is the children's ministry director for her church as well as a leader of a Christian women's organization. Katy and her husband are both born New Englanders, but have been known to travel at the drop of a hat. As her homeschooled kids say, they consider themselves "world-schooled." But no matter where Katy is you can always find her at www.katyleebooks.com. She would love to connect with you.

GRAVE DANGER
KATY LEE

HARLEQUIN® LOVE INSPIRED® SUSPENSE

Recycling programs
for this product may
not exist in your area.

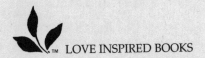 LOVE INSPIRED BOOKS

ISBN-13: 978-0-373-04209-8

GRAVE DANGER

www.Harlequin.com

Printed in U.S.A.

A capable, intelligent, and virtuous woman—
who is he who can find her?
She is far more precious than jewels
and her value is far above rubies.
Her husband has full confidence in her
and lacks nothing of value.
She brings him good, not harm,
all the days of her life.
　　　　　　　　—Proverbs 31:10–12

To Audrey, my oldest daughter
and Pinterest professional, I love having you
on my team, but what I love most is you.
I especially love your ambition to reach for the
stars. You call your blog Rd2Gold, but I want you
to always remember, with God as your goal, guide,
and guardian, your road is already paved with gold.
Trust Him, sweetie, and believe it.

Acknowledgments

I want to give my editor, Emily Rodmell,
a big thank you for her stellar visionary skills to
make the Love Inspired stories shine. Thank you,
Emily, for seeing something in my own writing
during the Happily Editor After Pitch Day, too!
This amazing opportunity has changed my life.

I also want to thank the Love Inspired readers
who collect our books. Thank you for
your wonderful notes of encouragement
and for your dedication to the LI line.

ONE

The dark, hollow eyes of a human skull put Sheriff Wesley Grant on the spot. The sockets, though vacant of life, were filled with questions he didn't have answers for. Unnerved by the skeleton's perpetual stare, he averted his gaze to the finger bones camouflaged against the gray pebbled sand. The digits protruded up as though the person had clawed their way out from their oceanfront grave. A grave that had no business being on this side of the island.

Wesley had questions of his own. "Who are you, and when did you get here?" The Maine island of Stepping Stones was his jurisdiction, and if this corpse was a recent death, then it was put here on his watch. Recent dumped bodies only meant one thing.

Homicide.

But who? One of his islanders?

The thought of these skeletal remains belonging to one of his charges squeezed his chest in a vise. The weight of that scenario bore down on him like the thick, dark clouds overhead. The April rains offered a reprieve, but the cold wind still whipped at his face. He ignored the chafing on his cheeks for the suffering the guy at his feet had to have experienced.

"Please don't let it be one of our own. I can't let these people down. Not when they've done so much for me. No, this can't be one of them." Wes pushed the horrid idea out of his mind as he pushed his windblown strands of hair out of his eyes. He would know if someone had gone missing. He ran a tight ship here, questioning every happening and every outsider who disembarked the Sunday ferry. This skeleton had to be ancient, put here long ago, before his time. Before his father's, the previous Sheriff Grant's, time. Before *any* of the islanders' time.

Wesley thought of the history of the island and remembered a couple hundred years ago, pirates used to sail these seas and stop off on the island to count their loot. Yes, that had to be it. He latched on to this theory quickly. This skeleton had to have been buried here by one of the eighteenth-century swashbucklers, killed by a warring foe who broached the shores. Wesley felt sure Dr. Simon Webber, the forensic anthropologist who would be arriving on the island any minute now, would confirm it. But a check of his watch only brought up another question: What was keeping the doctor?

Deputy Derek Vaughn had left over five hours ago to pick up the man the medical examiner was sending out here to assess the situation. Vaughn had been instructed to bring the forensic anthropologist over to this side of the island as soon as they arrived. It was a two-hour trip each way. That made Vaughn an hour late. Nothing new there. The deputy couldn't follow simple orders on a good day.

Wes thumbed the radio at his shoulder and called his other deputy, Owen Matthews. Maybe he knew what was keeping Vaughn. "Matthews, what's your location?"

The radio crackled in his ear as Wesley studied the skeleton's pelvis that lay exposed in the sand at his feet. Most of its ribs couldn't be seen, just the front of the rib cage protruded out of the earth. Only one hand stuck out, too. Wesley figured the other one was either still buried, or the wildlife had made off with it. Or, because the guy had once been a pirate—Wesley was sticking with this theory for the time being—there was the chance he'd lost it premortem.

The idea made him cringe and he pushed the radio again, a little harder than before. "Matthews or Vaughn, what's your twenty?"

His radio chirped followed by Deputy Matthews's voice. "Sorry, Wes. I'm pulling up now. Vaughn brought the doctor to the station instead. A little misunderstanding, I guess."

Wesley bit the unprofessional comment about Vaughn from his tongue and asked, "Where's the doctor?"

"She's sitting right beside me."

"She?" He spoke louder than he meant to, then remembered the boys who had found the skeleton that morning stood on the other side of the tall sand mound behind him. They didn't want to be near the "dead guy" as they'd put it. Their older sister, Pat, joined them as the responsible party, so she waited with them on the other side of the mound, too. None of these people needed to hear him lose his cool about an unexpected outsider showing up instead of the expected Dr. Webber.

"Yup. She's a she," Owen said. "Go a little easier on her than you did my wife when she showed up in Stepping Stones, would you?" Before the radio chirped out, Owen added, "I'm sure you've learned by now that not everyone is like Jenny Carmichael."

Owen was right. He also knew Wes had a hard time with outsiders. He'd put the last outsider who disembarked the ferry through the ringer. And Miriam Hunter, now Miriam Matthews, hadn't been guilty of anything but caring about Stepping Stones as much as he did.

Owen proved his point. Not all people who broached his shores were trouble. They weren't all like his ex-fiancée, Jenny Carmichael. Wesley recoiled at the memory of the destruction Jenny brought to his life five years ago, but that didn't mean the lady doctor was anything like Jenny.

He hoped she wasn't, anyway.

The motor of a boat beyond the sand mound signaled Matthews's arrival. Wes climbed the steep slope and got his first glimpse of the bone doctor sitting beside his deputy.

A pretty face behind dark-rimmed glasses. *So what?* A face meant nothing. He knew this from Jenny. *And don't you forget it, Grant,* he told himself as he approached the water and watched the brown-haired woman with a tight bun at the nape of her neck stand to her full, tower-like height. A pretty face *and* the height to go head-to-head with him.

That didn't necessarily mean trouble, he reasoned as this new outsider was about to broach his shores.

But even as Deputy Matthews slid out the metal gangway, the uncertainty in Wesley's mind rang louder than the screeching metal against metal.

All he could wonder was if this outsider would be friend or if she would be foe?

* * *

"I'm here to examine the skeleton." Lydia Muir stepped off the police boat and down the temporary metal dock Deputy Matthews slid out for her exit. She carried her tool kit in her left hand, her SLR digital camera hung from her neck, swaying with each step. She would hold off donning her forensic white coverall clean suit and rubber boots until she had the chance to assess the scene, but deep down under her grayish-blue wool coat and matching pants, Lydia squirmed in anticipation of suiting up. She hoped her excitement didn't show too much, pretty sure the five islanders standing in front of her wouldn't appreciate her smiling in their disturbing situation. They wouldn't understand that forensic anthropology, the study of human remains for evidence, was her life. A dug-up bone to the ordinary person was a treasure to behold for her.

"I'm Sheriff Grant." A shaggy-haired officer stepped forward. She didn't know too many officers of the law who kept their hair on the longer side. Most looked like the clean-cut deputy who brought her over to this side of the island, or the balding one who brought her out from Rockland. "I wasn't expecting you," the sheriff said in a disgruntled tone that had her putting aside her thoughts on his reclusive hairstyle and focusing on his obvious disappointment at her arrival.

Her excitement fizzled a bit. Apparently, he'd been expecting her boss.

"I'm Dr. Lydia Muir." She offered her hand to shake, glad to see him remove his black leather glove and take it. All hope wasn't lost yet.

The feeling of his warm grip seeped into her chilled skin, reminding her she should have brought gloves to this frigid, windswept place. She let go and felt the chill in the air more now than before. The first thought that jumped in her head was to take his warm hand in her own again. How silly, she thought, since she much preferred the company of the stiff and dead. But then, Sheriff Grant *was* pretty stiff. He gripped his jaw so tight, his temporomandibular joint protruded. The man was really mad that Webber wasn't here.

"I work under Dr. Simon Webber. He sent me in his stead." Lydia brought her tool kit in front of her to show the sheriff as well as all their onlookers that she had the credentials for being here. She cleared her throat. "I assure you, I'm well qualified to assess the situation. I have a Ph.D. in forensic anthropology, and I—" She bit the inside of her cheek to stop any more insecure blabbering from spilling forth. She had nothing to prove here. *I've earned this. I'm a doctor—even if Dr. Webber still calls me Miss Muir.*

But that would all change after this case. Running a top-notch examination here was exactly what she needed to prove herself in her field, once and for all. God had seen to it. He wanted her to succeed in her own right. Not because of who her father is in the world of science, but because of her own merits.

Lydia breathed deep and silently prayed. *God, You have given me the skills and the desire to understand the basic makeup and structure of Your creation. I am ready to handle whatever anyone, even the hard-faced sheriff giving himself TMJ, throws at me.*

She straightened all twenty-seven vertebrae of her spine and hoped the onlookers missed her trembling shoulders. *She* hoped they shook from the whipping wind and not nerves. "It's quite cold out here, and it looks like it could start to pour any second. Perhaps you can show me the crime scene now."

The sheriff's mouth twisted instantly. "*Crime scene?* Dr. Muir, it is way too soon to call this incident a crime. I'm sure this is nothing more than a historic burial unearthed by erosion."

Lydia blinked, speechless. She watched the wind lift the front of the man's blond, silky hair. Piercing blue eyes became exposed to her and chilled her more than the cold wind. His gaze narrowed on her face. A face she knew made her look younger than her thirty-three years. Her dad always said, despite her height, she had a baby face, and in times like this his nickname, "Trinket," would do nothing for her credibility. Not that it ever did, but that never stopped him from using it.

"Perhaps you are right about the remains being ancient," she said, treading carefully.

"I'm sorry if I made the wrong assumption. I was told a skeleton had been found. The M.E. asked my department for a consultation, and Dr. Webber sent me—"

Saying the words out loud made her realize how ridiculous they sounded. Out of all her other colleagues, Webber had sent *her?*

What was left of her excitement fizzled out completely as she realized what this really meant. She could have kicked one of the stones at her feet. Webber sent her for the same reasons this guy spouted. Dr. Webber didn't want to make the trek out to the cold north for old ancient remains. That's why he told her to box them up and bring them back to him. She was nothing more than a courier of goods. And here she thought she might finally have earned Dr. Webber's support for the promotion to Director of Anthropology.

Lydia squelched her rising disappointment. She could dwell on it later when she was alone. For now, regardless of why she was sent here, she would see the case through professionally. She would not make any judgment until she had assessed the scene. With her chin lifted a notch, she met Sheriff Grant at eye level, thankful her tight bun didn't allow the wind to play peekaboo with her strands like his. She had one chance to set the stage and show she meant business.

Lydia pushed her glasses up on her nose—and noticed his deprecatory eyes travel down her tall body. Her bravado faltered as she realized he formed judgments of her. Terms from her childhood, and even adulthood, came to mind. Beanpole. Giraffe. Sunshade. At least her six-one-and-then-some height wouldn't be blocking any sun on the island today, because there was none.

"Just show me the way," she said, and caught the other people behind the sheriff staring.

"Not until I have your word that you will keep this discreet," Sheriff Grant said, pulling her attention back to him. "I'm not looking for some fresh-out-of-college intern looking to make headlines or improve herself in her profession. I want your word that you're not here to further your career or to make a name for yourself."

"Further my—?" She sputtered to a stop. *How did he know?* She attempted to keep her face as still as the granite ledges around her, but her shoulders trembled all on their own. Was it the cold, or was she that transparent?

"It's my job to protect the islanders from harm," Sheriff Grant continued. "I need to know you can be discreet and professional."

"Always," she answered quickly, but her voice held a shiver. It had to be the cold and not fear. Never fear. With God as her guide, never shall she fear.

The sheriff's unnerving, steely eyes relaxed a little, but not his jaw. "Good to hear, but tell me, Doc, did you think to bring a coat? It gets real chilly out here with the wind and all. The climate is a bit rougher than what you're used to on the mainland."

"Of course I brought a coat. It's in my bag on the boat. But I'm perfectly comfortable as I am." She ignored the cold, salty spray misting around her, knowing it would seep into her wool suit real fast. Now, *there* was a smell to avoid. Death she could handle, but wet sheep, not so much.

"Your shaking shoulders tell me differently, but have it your way." He shrugged as he tossed a glance over his shoulder at two gawking teenaged boys huddled together. "These boys are Robbie and Mack Reed." Neither would pass for fifteen. Their faces were pale and sullen with eyes as turbulent as the waves behind them.

Their timorous behavior told her these young ones were her body finders.

Sheriff Grant confirmed her assessment. "They came out to this side of the island earlier this morning to explore and came across the skeleton."

Lydia scanned the backdrop of rocky ledges. She wondered how much farther the island expanded beyond them. Stone surrounded her, from the rocky ledges to the numerous flat rocks dotting the ocean behind her. They couldn't have been more strategically placed if they had been pawns on a chess board with the island of Stepping Stones as their queen. A lighthouse stood far out in the distance on the farthest rock, warning ships not to come any closer to the dangerous protruding stones. A natural tactic that seemingly kept the outside world at bay, and the town untouchable.

Until now.

"Do people come here often?" she asked.

The sheriff hesitated before he answered, "We don't get too many visitors in Stepping Stones. Or did you mean this side of the island?"

"Both."

He shrugged. "Most stay on the side where the higher ground is. These waters get pretty rough. Storms come through and submerge these rocks real fast." He angled a disappointed look at the boys. Their chins dropped lower to their chests; apparently, they had already heard the lecture. "The boys know they made a dangerous choice today, but I think under the circumstances they've been punished enough."

Their punishment, *her* reward. Just thinking about digging her hands into the dirt had Lydia's adrenaline spiking again. She took a breath and piped up. "Okay, boys, show me what you found."

Mouths gaped. The boys' visible gulps said they weren't too excited about their find—or finding it again anytime soon. The one named Robbie retreated behind his brother, shaking his head. He looked to Mack, who had another year or so on him, to take the lead.

A little empathy, she reminded herself. It's not every day kids see a dead body. Never mind a decomposed one. This was why she didn't do well in social situations. People didn't "get" her excitement, and she tended to forget her brain worked differently than most. "It's okay," she assured the boys, "just point the way. I'll take it from here."

The one named Mack flipped his red hair off to his left. His hands stuffed into his zipped-up gray sweatshirt. "I found...*it*...over there when I pulled our rowboat up onshore. At first, I thought they were sticks. Then I saw the sk—skull." He visibly shivered. A woman came up beside him to drape her arm around his shoulders and pull him close. Her carrot-red hair matched that of the boys. She looked too young to be their mother, but definitely related. Lydia was about to ask when the woman plastered pleading hazel eyes on the sheriff.

"Wes, can I please take them home now? They've told you everything they know. It's bad enough they had to be the ones to find... the body."

Lydia watched the woman's eyes fill with a level of intimacy as they locked on the sheriff's. The two of them must be an item, she speculated, but the sheriff's blank and emotionless stare implied Lydia failed on that assessment. *Not a good start, Dr. Muir.*

Sheriff Grant turned to her. "Do you need to ask them anything, Doc?"

"If I do, I'm sure I can find them easy enough," Lydia answered.

"True, but I want this matter wrapped up today."

Lydia studied him and wondered about the rush. The bones weren't going anywhere. "I'll take your requested expedience into consideration, but I won't make any promises."

He shot her a disapproving look but signaled the dark-haired deputy. "Matthews, would you mind bringing Pat and the boys home? I'll take Dr. Muir back in my patrol boat."

"I'll put her bag in your boat," the deputy replied, and unhooked a set of keys from his belt.

"Thanks. I don't know how long I'm going to be." He lowered his voice below the pounding of the waves and squawking seagulls, but not so low that Lydia couldn't hear what he said. "It looks like it might be a while."

"That will all depend on what I dig up," Lydia announced as she took a step in the direction Mack had insinuated with his head toss.

"What you dig up?" Sheriff Grant balked as she walked past him. "Hold on a minute. You're not turning this place into a dig site."

She kept on walking. A few moments later a boat's engine rumbled to life, leaving her with the sheriff on this side of the island. Each of her footsteps was carefully placed on the squishy mounds of sand. Either it had just poured or when the tide came in, the water surely covered this side of the island.

Which would explain the unearthing of the body over time. But how much time? A hundred years? Or one?

Thoughts of the skeleton had her picking up her step. How long had it been here? What was the cause of death? What was its ancestry? Why was it buried on this side alone, and what were the secrets it took to its shallow grave? All things forensic science could answer—all things she could answer. Lydia hurried forward, eager to locate the remains, and eager to find what they would tell her.

After another ten yards, the lay of the land dropped considerably beneath her shoes. The backs of her calves tightened in an effort to keep her from sliding down on her rump. That would be the icing on the sheriff's cake. She could have no mishaps with this case. She didn't doubt he would be the first to call Dr. Webber to get her out of here. He seemed as territorial as a bulldog. She wondered what he had to guard…or perhaps hide.

The ground sloped more. Lydia turned to crab-walk down a steep mound of sand. With her feet solidly planted, she took the next sidestep. Then her gaze caught on the protruding rib cage sticking out of the sand, and all thoughts of the bulldog vanished.

She took her next step without looking down and felt her feet slip beneath her. Her arms shot out to catch her balance, but her tool kit unevenly distributed her weight and she slipped more, dropping her case and picking up speed as she descended. In a crouch, she locked her legs to stop the slide, but there was no way out of it. She was going down. In mere seconds, she would find herself cuddled up with the skeletal remains of an adult female.

"Do you always get so up close and personal with your work, Doc?" Wes gripped the upper arm of the bone hunter. He caught her midair, pulling her back like a rag doll. A very tall and thin rag doll.

"All the time," she boasted. Her shaking fingers tugged at the bottom of her suit coat. For a doctor, she wasn't very bright to come out to the cold north with no gloves. She probably only had the latex variety in her black case.

Wes noticed her tool kit a few feet down the embankment. She'd dropped it in her fall. He sidestepped down to retrieve it, not sure why he did. He shouldn't be helping her in any way. Not until he knew if she intended to sensationalize the find or not. He dared not tell her about the pirates. If word got out, he'd have every treasure hunter in the Northeast invading his island by morning.

His best choice would be to stick close and hurry her up. Wes handed the kit over and watched her grip the hard case at her front as she'd done before. A buffer between them, perhaps? A means of protection? "I'm not going to hurt you," he chided.

"I didn't think you were." Her coffee-colored eyes widened to saucer size through her lenses.

"Then what's with—" Wes shook it off. "Forget it. Let's just get this over with so we can get out of the cold. The sun's setting."

"Sun?" She looked to the skies without a squint.

He did a double take. Was this woman being snarky with him? "Yeah, sun." He tapped his watch. "Five-thirty. Daylight is disappearing while we stand here over this dead guy."

"Girl." She looked straight at him.

"What?"

"It's a dead girl. Woman actually."

"How do you know?"

"Her posterior ramus of the mandible is straighter than that of a male's."

"I see." He didn't have a clue.

"A male's is much more curved."

"Right." He scratched at the back of his neck. "Is that all?"

"Well, a woman's pelvis is wider, as well."

"Of course, but can you give me an estimate of age?"

The doctor turned away to give the skeleton her full attention. Wes watched how Lydia Muir became absorbed in her task to the point where he thought she forgot he still stood behind her. Minutes went by while she dropped her case at her feet and opened it to withdraw a pair of blue latex gloves. She approached the bones and crouched down.

Her hand reached out, tracing some markings on the ribs. Abruptly, she stood and circled around to the other side with continued skilled concentration.

"Well?" Wesley reminded her of his presence.

"Well…" She bit her lower lip. "Judging by the slight pitting and sharpness of her ribs at her sternal area, I would estimate her age between twenty-five and thirty years when she died."

"I meant the age of the bones. Are they ancient or are they fresh?"

"I can't answer that without a full examination."

"And what does that entail?"

"It means sectioning this site off to search for any clothing, jewelry or artifacts that might give me a ballpark date of burial."

"Too long. I need something to go by now."

She scooped a handful of sand away from the pelvis area. A few more scoops and she pulled up something rusty. "How about a zipper? Not your typical *ancient* woman's attire."

The doctor grabbed a plastic bag from her

case, but before she dropped it in the bag, she placed it back where she found it and snapped a picture of it with her camera. Then she stood and handed him the bag with the zipper in it to study.

"I'm going to need more proof than a zipper to tell me that we're not dealing with an old corpse. Zippers have been around for at least a century."

Dr. Muir met him at eye level. She really was quite tall if she came close to his six-five height. Even if they were nearly equal in height, they weren't in width. With her hands on her slim waist, elbows jutting out at her side in sharp points, she looked as though the whipping wind could take her for a ride.

"Sheriff, I won't be able to determine her age until I get the remains back to my lab and analyze their nitrogen level. The higher the level, the younger the age. Anything younger than twenty years will require an investigation, whether you like it or not."

"You seem pretty smart, Doc. Surely you have something in that kit of yours that can push this along. Give you one of those ball-parks you mentioned."

Dr. Muir pinched her trembling and pur-pling lips, reminding him that she wasn't as smart as he gave her credit for. The fool woman didn't even know how to dress ade-quately for the climate, and now the cold was settling into her own bones.

Wesley ripped off his coat. "Put this on be-fore you freeze."

She questioned him with raised eyebrows, but her lips relaxed at his offer. She took his heavy uniform coat without a fight and quickly stuffed her arms into the sleeves and zipped up.

She went back to her tool kit. "I suppose it's getting dark enough that I could use my ultra-violet flashlight to give you a guess, but this is off the record. I won't put it in writing." She turned back with a small black flashlight. "Fresh bones glow a blue color under UV light. Time causes the fluorescence to dimin-ish from the outside in, giving a relative age at each stage of glowing. Bones older than a hundred years won't glow at all." She clicked the light on and beamed it on the skull.

Neither of them said anything as vivid blue fluoresced, illuminating the facial features straight through. Wesley pinched the bridge of his nose at the truth staring back at him. He didn't need the doctor to state anything off the record. And denying the facts wouldn't change them. These weren't pirate bones, and treasure hunters were the least of his worries. These bones were fresh ones buried in a shallow grave.

The doctor looked up from her crouched position. "Less than ten years, and these markings on the rib cage—" she pointed at the tiny lines "—are lacerations made by a knifelike instrument. It would appear a crime has occurred on your island, Sheriff Grant. And my assessment says it's murder."

TWO

"Dr. Webber, I'm certain these bones are less than ten years old." Lydia spoke quietly into her cell phone from the back porch of Deputy Matthews's home, where he and his wife had generously offered to put Lydia up for the night.

Stepping Stones didn't have a hotel or a motel or any type of boardinghouse really. If it weren't for their offer, Lydia would have been sleeping in one of the two cells at the sheriff's station. This huge captain's house perched on the top of a ledge overlooking the sea, capped with its own widow's walk and porches, was much better digs. Mrs. Matthews even offered her a lovely room with an ocean view, and Lydia knew come daylight when she could see it, she would love it even more.

Lydia faced the black sea and continued her conversation. "I also see evidence of multiple lacerations on the rib cage. This looks like a murder, and I'm recommending a full investigation."

"You will do nothing of the sort," Simon Webber grumbled nasally. "Your job was to assess the situation and report back to me. *I* will determine if an investigation is in order. You have not been authorized, Miss Muir."

"It's *Doctor* Muir, and you authorized me to make this call when you sent me here."

"My mistake. It won't happen again. Unfortunately, I am still detained with museum business. Tag and categorize the remains and bring them back to me. I'll determine if the coroner needs to be called in. You are not to call him."

"Sir, I am not an intern any longer. I—"

"Bring the remains to me, Miss Muir. Or you will regret it."

The phone went dead, and Lydia heaved a sigh. She leaned forward against the railing and blew out her frustration. Waves roared over and over in the dark night. The sound lulled her as she angled her head over her shoulder and eyed Deputy Matthews and Sheriff Grant through the doorway to the kitchen.

They stood around the breakfast island conversing in their own hushed tones and using sign language for the benefit of the deputy's deaf wife, also leaning against the yellow Formica countertop. Lydia pulled her coat tighter around her to ward off the slicing air and pocketed the phone.

Her lips pressed tight to regain her composure before facing the officers with the change of plans. As it turned out, this wasn't her big break after all. It wasn't her time to shine. God had not prepared her way here as she'd thought. Today would end no differently than any other. More than anything Lydia wanted to fade out of Deputy Matthews's home. She didn't want to have to tell them she'd been trumped. Again.

But she couldn't let them see her failure. Professionalism through and through. That's the way it had to be. Always, and under every circumstance. She would not let Dr. Webber break her down. She'd come this far with all his comparisons, pitting her against her father. As if she'd ever win that prize. She'd accepted a long time ago that she would never be as brilliant as the great scientist, her father, Dr. Gerard Muir. Apparently Dr. Webber thought she *would* be when he hired her.

If only she could show him what she was capable of with this case. She may not be her father, but if he would give her a chance, he would see she was a good forensic anthropologist. He would see she was a good candidate for the directorship position. If only.

Lydia breathed deep and exhaled a condensed cloud of air into the cold night, accepting the position wasn't to be so for her.

"Problem?"

Lydia whipped around to find Sheriff Grant standing there. *How long had* he *been there?*

"Everything's fine," she blurted out and averted her eyes to look at the lit hurricane lantern hanging on the doorframe adjacent to his head.

"Liar."

"Excuse me?" Lydia stepped back into the

porch railing, reaching for anything to separate her from this too-good-looking bulldog. She settled for her hands on her abdomen. She knew his kind. He was probably a jock in high school who steered clear of the brainy girls—*if* he noticed them at all.

"You look beaten." Through his long strands of hair, he eyed her fidgeting hands, and she stilled them. "Did Boss Man change your plans?"

Lydia raised her chin a bit, but then chose truth over bravado. "You'll be happy to know I won't be digging on your precious island tomorrow. Dr. Webber has requested I take the skeleton back to the lab for a consult to determine age in the lab with the right equipment. However, I would like the area to be protected until the report is finished. Just in case."

"Why isn't he coming?"

"He's consulting for a museum."

"Museum consulting." The sheriff's jaw ticked. The man was going to grind down his molars if he didn't learn to relax a little. "Look, Doc, I don't see how some pharaoh's tomb, or whatever is keeping him, is more important than this. I need to assure the islanders their home is safe. It would appear Dr. Webber doesn't think Stepping Stones is worth the trip, so I would like for you to identify this skeleton before you leave."

"I have to decline."

"And why's that?"

"Because…because I'll lose my job."

"How about off the record, then? You know you can't leave us here in good conscience with no answers."

Lydia bit her lower lip. Returning to her lab would mean handing this case over to Webber or, worse, one of the others to solve. But staying on Stepping Stones could kill her career completely.

And why should she trust this man anyway? He didn't trust her. She had to be crazy to even be considering this. "I'll lose my job," she whispered more to herself, and wondered if she already hadn't. What would her father say then?

"I'm sure that's a possibility, Doc," Sheriff Grant stated quietly, and pushed his mussed-up hair out of his eyes. She noticed his intense blues soften in the lantern light. She also noticed the way her fingers twitched when he cleared away his hair. Shock smacked her in the chest as she realized she'd wanted to reach up and do the same.

But then Sheriff Grant's words stopped any thoughts of touching his hair. He understood the risk she would be taking by staying to help him. Lydia pressed her lips. Her decision would determine the path for the rest of her career, even life. And following this man whom she didn't know in the least might lead her to never work again.

Or maybe this was the path God had prepared for her all along. Maybe this skeleton was God's way of boosting her career. Maybe this was her chance to prove she was capable. Prove it to Webber, and prove it to her father.

She prayed silently for God's direction, but she also knew she could only stay and work with Wesley Grant if he was a believer. "Are you a Christian?" she asked him straight out.

Sheriff Grant hesitated, and she thought he would say no. The words practically molded to his lips, but something stopped him from voicing them. His bullishness faded a bit, and he said, "I used to be. Why?"

Lydia breathed a little easier at his answer. It wasn't an outright *no.* This really could be her ticket for an upgrade, after all. "Before I decide to team up with you, I want to make sure we have the same guide."

"And if we don't?"

"But we do. Even if you've given up on God during this time of your life, He hasn't given up on you. He's still leading you."

"I highly doubt it. When my parents died within two years of each other, I considered God dead to me, too. But if it makes you stay, you can believe whatever you like."

"I believe you still belong to Him, so for that reason, you can count me in, Sheriff." A bit of fear mixed with a jolt of excitement coursed through her at the sound of her agreeable words springing from her lips. She felt a hesitant smile form as Sheriff Grant extended his hand to shake. Lydia reached for it and verbalized her confounding thoughts. "I've never done anything so insensible. My career could end up in the same condition as the skeleton. Dead." *Or it could skyrocket.*

Whatever Your will, let it be, God. With that, Lydia shook Sheriff Grant's hand with conviction. "Let's do it. Let's identify this woman."

As she gave his hand a few good pumps, she noticed how it enveloped her thin-boned one with triple the size and strength. Sheriff Wesley Grant was one strong man and could overpower her in an instant. The thought caused a little fear of him to sprout. Perhaps losing her job shouldn't be her only concern. Doubts flickered in her mind about this man with whom she'd just struck a deal. Should she have done a little digging into the life of Wesley Grant before she signed over anyone's death certificate to him?

Sheriff Grant's piercing blue eyes peeked through his blond strands again. She got the feeling he was questioning her sincerity, too. Seconds ticked by while she made the decision to fully trust him. She let go and decided only time would tell.

"I'm sure I don't have to tell you your island

isn't as safe as you think," Lydia said, breaking their analyzing silence. "Someone may not want this body found, and that someone is most likely one of your islanders. Other people could be in danger."

He nodded solemnly. "I agree the islanders could be in danger, but I can't believe one of our own did this." His tough voice from before was now threaded with sadness. "Meet me at 8:00 a.m. at the Underground Küchen Restaurant on the pier. Time is critical. I can't and won't let harm come to this island or its people. I owe them that much."

"Owe them? For what?"

Sheriff Grant turned and grabbed the handle to the screen door. "Let's just say I had my own little brush with the law once. Someone tried to pin a theft on me. The islanders believed in me when no one else did, and for that, I owe them."

How do you sign "Thank you"? Lydia scrawled out her message on the pad of paper Miriam Matthews carried with her to help her converse with the hearing world.

The woman's golden-red hair draped prettily around her elegant face as she bent to read the note from behind the wheel of her SUV. The deaf woman had given Lydia a ride into town on her way to the high school where she worked as the school's principal. A smile blossomed on her lips when she lifted her pretty face. She brought her right-hand fingertips to her mouth, then pulled her hand straight out in front of her to demonstrate the sign.

Lydia mimicked the hand motion a few times until she got it right. She wanted to say, "Thank you for the ride," but with no knowledge of American Sign Language, she had to settle for only "Thank you." She made a mental note to buy and memorize a sign-language book.

As she reached for the door handle to exit, the breathtaking view out her passenger window caused her to linger. Beyond the boardwalk and its quaint gray clapboard shops was a long wooden pier reaching out to the expansive, shimmering sea. Sharp rocks with spraying swells dotted the water far below the pier. From inside the car, she could hear their steady, rushing sounds that lulled her into a state of reflection—specifically for what might happen to this secluded gem of a land when word got out someone had been brutally murdered.

Miriam tapped her on the shoulder, pulling her out of her thoughts. Her pad of paper had a message scrawled across the top. *Do you like the ocean?*

"I could listen to it for hours." Lydia winced and hoped Miriam couldn't read lips. Here she was, speaking about hearing the ocean, and Miriam couldn't hear a thing. *Empathy, Lydia. Empathy.*

Miriam scribbled out another message, *I understand,* and Lydia's shoulders sagged in embarrassment. The woman *could* read lips.

Lydia took the pad and pen to write quickly *I'm sorry. I didn't mean—*

Miriam snatched the pad away, her head shaking back and forth, a reassuring smile on her lightly freckled face. "It's…all right." Mrs. Matthews spoke aloud, her voice a little squeaky but articulate. "I imagine…

the sound is beautiful." Her face lit up in a friendly, reassuring smile while her hands made the signs for her words. The word for beautiful was represented by Miriam's long fingers fanning out in a sweeping circle over her whole face. Lydia didn't think she'd ever seen anything more beautiful. Immediately, her hand went to her face to practice the sign, determined to learn it right away.

"I can see you love to learn," Miriam said again. "That tells me...you are good at your job."

Lydia's practicing hand stilled over her face. How did this woman know those were the words she'd longed to hear for the last five years?

For some unknown reason, this woman who couldn't hear a word didn't need words to see deep into people and connect with them. Miriam must make a great principal here on the island. Lydia thought the kids must love this kind, perceptive and encouraging lady.

For the first time in her life, Lydia didn't feel pressured to come up with small talk, and yet, all she wanted to do was talk and get to know Miriam Matthews. And couldn't. The language barrier would stand in the way. Another reason for the book. She'd order it today.

A knock on the passenger window whipped Lydia's head to her right. It was the balding deputy who had picked her up in Rockland yesterday and brought her to Stepping Stones. She rolled down the window. "Good morning, Deputy Vaughn, how are you?"

"Morning, Doctor. I'm doing well, thank ya. I just left the site. Kept watch over the remains all night for you, just like you asked. And call me Derek. We're not formal around here."

"I have a feeling Sheriff Grant would disagree with you on that one. He seems like a by-the-book kind of guy, but okay, Derek, thank you for protecting the scene."

The man's brown beady eyes darkened. Had she said something wrong? "It wouldn't be the first time the sheriff and I have disagreed," he grumbled deeply.

Lydia fidgeted in her seat. There were obviously some unresolved issues going on at the sheriff's station between Sheriff Grant and his deputy. Lydia knew how that went, having issues with her own boss. This was empathy she could offer. "I'm sorry to hear that, Derek. I know work relationships can be difficult."

"For sure." His thick Maine accent made her smile. He seemed like a nice man. "Do you need a ride over to the site?" he asked.

"No, I'm meeting Sheriff Grant at the Underground Küchen. He'll bring me, but thank you."

The man shrugged his rounded shoulders and pulled out a pair of leather gloves. "I'll just head back to the station and do some paperwork then. That's all I'm ever allowed to do, anyway." Derek pivoted to his left and disappeared around the back of the car.

The two women watched him in the rearview mirrors disappear behind a gray clapboard shack with multicolored lobster buoys hanging off the side.

Lydia swung back around to Miriam with a shrug. "Looks like the sheriff has caused some strife with his deputy. I can't say I'm surprised. He's been a little rude to me, too."

Miriam frowned for a moment before picking up her pad and pen. After a minute, she passed the pad over. *Wesley cares about the islanders more than anything. I know he can be hard on people, but that's only because people have been hard on him. When I first came here, he was horrible to me. I have forgiven him, and knowing what I know now about him, I hurt for him.*

Lydia read the note, but all she could do was nod and look out to sea. Bad things happen to people. That didn't give them the right to pay the pain forward. And she would make sure the sheriff knew that the next time he barked at her.

Lydia smiled politely and stepped out, turning to sign "thank you" again.

Miriam scrawled another message and held out the pad with a twinkle in her eyes. *Don't order the special. It feeds an army. Owen once made that mistake, and it wasn't pretty.*

An image of the deputy stuffing his face with a whole lot of knockwurst made Lydia giggle. It lightened her mood as she hefted her tool kit to the place she was supposed to meet the sheriff.

Down the street and onto the boardwalk, a row of stores and restaurants welcomed her.

The two restaurants were on either end of the boardwalk with a long row of storefronts and alleyways sandwiched between them. The Underground Küchen was closest to her and built right into the side of one of the rocky cliffs. She stepped up to the glass window, intrigued to find out if she could see the cliff inside on the back wall.

She couldn't see a cliff, but she did see hoards of people inside. Breakfast at the Underground Küchen bustled, and her stomach went all queasy at the sight. She had to go in there and converse with all those people. She'd never been good at basic conversation. She'd much rather talk about the molecular makeup of the human body, but most people glazed over as soon as she said the words *chemical composition*.

Had the sheriff arrived yet? She hoped so and searched for Wesley's long, silky strands in the crowd. At the sight of her silly grin in the reflection of the glass, she backed away from the window and headed to a wooden bench. She couldn't believe how girlish she was acting over the surly man. Even if he was a very *beautiful,* surly man.

Lydia imagined the tall, strong sheriff and practiced her newly acquired hand sign for the word *beautiful* as she moved toward the bench. Just as she was about to sit, her arm was yanked back as her tool kit was nearly ripped from her hands.

She whipped around, tightening her hold on the handle with every ounce of muscle in her. As she wrenched her case back, she took notice of a pair of black leather gloves on the thief's hands. Gloves that resembled the ones the sheriff had worn yesterday.

The person pulled harder, but Lydia held on as though a life depended on it. And it did. Hers. Without her tool kit, she couldn't do her job.

She raised her gaze to see who she fought so hard, but all she caught was the pulled down bill of a black baseball cap. Big black sunglasses covered more than half of her assailant's tilted-down face. She wanted to rip the hat off, but getting her tool kit took precedence.

With all her might, Lydia pulled up. In the same moment, her arm was yanked forward. She refused to let go and gave one more yank back. The force sent her body twisting and flying back into the air, the case out in front of her, still attached to her hand and leading the way.

She had no time to think more on it as her time of flying airborne came to an end after mere seconds. She fell hard on the splintery planks of the boardwalk, her chin taking the brunt of the fall, her teeth jarring in her mouth.

But the pain had to wait because her tool kit kept moving!

On the impact of her landing, she'd let go! The case that contained everything she needed flew from her hand and now skid-ded away from her on the wood—heading straight for the edge of the pier and the sharp rocks far below.

Lydia pushed up on her hands and knees and scrambled across as fast as she could to save it. Tears pricked her eyes as the edge drew near. She couldn't lose her kit. Dr. Webber would kill her. Or at least humiliate her to no end. He would be sure to note that her father would never make such a mishap.

Lydia threw herself into the air to make one final leap at catching the case before it disappeared into the ocean. She landed hard on her elbows, the case centimeters from her grasping fingertips. The kit continued to approach the edge, and just as she was about to watch it disappear, a black boot came down hard, cracking the wooden planks and stopping the kit dead in its tracks.

"Fall again, Doc?" a man's voice called from above, halting her scrambles. The only person who called her Doc was the sheriff. Slowly, she lifted her gaze from the boot in her face for confirmation.

"Did you attack me?" she asked, looking up and down the empty boardwalk. Then looked for his gloves. Bare hands. But he could have taken them off.

"Attack you? No. I just walked down from the road and saw you going after your case. You didn't fall?"

Lydia stood on shaky legs, her case held close to her chest. She shook her head in answer to his question and observed various pain points settling in. "Someone tried to steal my case. I managed to stop them, but in the process got thrown to the ground."

"Stay here," Sheriff Grant said in his deep, commanding voice, but somehow it sounded more comforting to her now. He ran down to the other end of the walk, looking into the alleyways as he passed them. After a few minutes of searching, he came back with palms up. "I don't see anyone."

"Well, I'm not making it up."

"If you say so, Doc."

"Well, I do." Lydia hiked up her case, perturbed with this guy's quick switch from helpful to skeptic. "I'm not lying," she huffed. Something in the sheriff's life made him really distrustful, and that was too bad, but she wasn't here to fix it. She was here for one thing only. "Can we just get started?"

"Don't you want breakfast?"

Lydia glanced at the restaurant. "It's too crowded. There's not an empty table anywhere in there."

"Doesn't matter if there was an empty table, you wouldn't be seated at it. That's not the way Tildy runs the place. Nobody sits alone."

"Tildy?" Lydia rubbed her throbbing elbows, grateful her plushy parka absorbed some of the shock.

He stopped in front of the glass door. "The owner. And the local news reporter." He made quotation marks with his fingers around *news reporter.* "You want to know something about the goings-on here on the island, all you have to do is ask Tildy. She'll be happy to explain it all to you. And I mean all." He opened the door and waved a hand. "After you, Doc."

"Lydia," she corrected him, not moving from her place. "My name is Lydia."

He paused for a few beats. "All right. I guess since we'll be working together, first names are fine. I'm Wes." He waved again for her to enter.

Her knees locked and her heart rate sped up. She could hear her own breathing and it didn't sound so good.

"What's the matter, Doc…uh, Lydia?" He shut the door.

"Nothing. It's just—"

"Just what?"

"I—I don't do well in crowds. I think I want to try the other place." She jutted her burning, scraped chin in the direction of the restaurant at the end of the boardwalk.

"The Blue Lobster isn't open for breakfast. Plus, I think there'll be a lot of people disappointed if the island's first anthropologist visitor didn't come to be welcomed appropriately."

"What's the big deal? I'm not some spectacle at the zoo."

His hands went up surrender-style. "Whoa, I didn't say you were, Doc. They're good people. I know they'll want to meet you. Come on. I'm going in with you."

"I don't know you any more than them."

He smiled a Cheshire Cat grin. "You're right. Maybe I should hold off introducing you and sell tickets in a big-top tent. I could put out flyers inviting one and all to the greatest spec—"

"Stop it, Wesley."

He froze. His icy blue irises pierced her through his long strands. His Adam's apple bobbed a couple times before he jerked a nod. "Sorry."

"You know, I'm not even hungry. Let's get over to the site and get set up. Did you get access to the list of supplies I gave to Owen? The tent and boxes?"

"Already been delivered. Owen's there now getting ready. We can head over right after I grab a bite to go." He peered through the glass door. "You can wait here if you want."

Lydia looked down the boardwalk for the man who tried to steal her tool kit. Her decision came swift.

She went inside.

What she thought should only take thirty seconds turned into ten minutes. She stood by the door while customers smiled at her as warmly as the fire blazing in the stone hearth at the back of the restaurant. Wood beams

and the old country with the friendly cama-
raderie relaxed her anxious nerves of crowds.
She found herself smiling back at the islanders, but still not sure of what to say.

Lydia looked for Wesley and found him behind the bar pouring his coffee and talking
to a young waitress dressed in a cobalt-blue
dirndl dress. Lydia knew the garment's tech-
nical name, having done her dissertation in
Germany. The white front laces and apron
shone brightly against the vivid velour—but
not as brightly as the girl's smile aimed at
Wesley. Someone was sweet on someone. But
then, Lydia couldn't blame the girl. Lydia had
looked the same way when she'd caught her
reflection in the window before.

"How do you take your coffee?" Wesley
called to her. "Sugar, cream?"

"Black, one sugar," Lydia answered.

The swinging doors at the back of the restaurant burst wide. An older woman with a
pouf of frizzy, bleached-blond hair bounced
out. "A girl after my own heart," she announced as she zigzagged through the maze
of tables and patrons until she stood in front

of Lydia. "Strong, but a little sweet. Hiya, I'm Tildy, and you must be the anthropologist. I've never met an anthropologist before. To be honest, it sounds a little creepy to me, but please come sit. Tell us all about it."

Wesley saved her. "Actually, Tildy, we can't stay. We're eating while we work today," he informed her as he passed Lydia a tall white to-go coffee cup and a brown paper bag of some kind of food.

"Oh, right. Those boys found some pirate bones, I hear."

"Pirate?" Lydia questioned. Was that what everyone thought? Then she remembered Wesley's statement about protecting the islanders. He must have told them the bones might be ancient. "Could be," she said, going along with it, suddenly not wanting to upset anyone here in this comforting and homey atmosphere, either.

"Wesley, don't work this lovely lady too hard. And be sure to bring her back for lunch. I think once you taste what's in the bag, you'll be back for more." She winked at Lydia and touched her hand that held the bag. Her gentle touch felt motherly and gave Lydia's heart pangs. It had been twenty years since she felt her mother's touch. Her breath caught at the unexpected pain of loss, but she smiled through it at this woman who looked at her with such openness. These were the good people Wesley was trying to protect.

"I'll be back," Lydia promised, and meant it as she let Wesley lead her out the door.

They walked in silence for a few minutes, then Wesley snatched the bag from her hand. "Are you ready for this? Tildy makes a great apple strudel." He removed a flaky pastry from the bag and took a bite, then held it out in front of her mouth. "Go ahead. You'll love it."

Lydia hesitated with a little shock. Never had she eaten from someone's hand. It felt so personal and intimate. Butterflies fluttered about in her stomach. *You're making too much of this,* she told herself. *It's just a bite of pastry. Not even from the same side he bit from. Just take a bite.*

Lydia opened her mouth to the sweet. She meant to take a nibble, but Wesley pushed a little more in her mouth and she ended up with a generous amount. "Mmm. This *is* good." She licked a smudge of apple filling from the corner of her lips and dived back in for another bite.

He laughed, a rich deep sound. "If you could see your face."

"What about my face?" she asked while still chewing.

"I guess there's a good reason Tildy calls them her German delights. Your face is quite delighted."

"Well, it's good. Real good."

"Told you so." He held up his coffee cup and took a sip, reminding her of her own delicious drink in her hand.

She sipped carefully of the rich molten lava. "Mmm. Perfect." She licked the nutty flavor from her lips. "I can see why you come here."

"Wait till you see what she gives you for lunch. It's because of her that I'm so healthy." He patted his belly, or non-belly, from what she could see. The man was sure fit.

"She takes good care of you, does she?"

"Especially since my mom died."

That's right. He said he lost both his parents. "Oh, I'm sorry. When—?"

"Eight years ago. No big deal. We should get going. You ready?" The swift subject change told her he might not mind sharing his pastry, but all intimacies ended there. He continued. "No roads lead to that part of the island, so we're taking the boat. I see you don't have gloves still. You can wear mine."

The sight of the black leather gloves he held out to her stumped her. The image of the gloved man who had tried to take her kit flashed before her eyes. Were they the same pair? She reached for the soft leather but couldn't be sure. They were sure alike.

"Do you want to drive the boat?"

Her head shot up, gloves forgotten. "Really? Are you sure? I'd love to, but I've never driven a boat before."

"You should probably learn, then, in case I'm not available to bring you over to the site."

If her hands were free she would have clapped. She settled for smiling big. "Let's do it."

Wesley smirked. "I've never seen any-one get so excited about driving a boat. You look ready to burst. When you grow up on an island, piloting a boat isn't a big thing."

"Well, I think it's pretty exciting."

Within minutes his sheriff's boat zipped them away from shore with Lydia beside him, memorizing every piece of equipment and direction he threw at her. "You're a fast learner, Doc," he yelled over the motor. "Hold on while I get us through the rocks, and then I'll give you the wheel!" Even though he smirked from the helm, his concentration was fully on maneuvering around the huge flat rocks sporadically jutting out of the water's surface. Danger signs bounced on buoys all around, warning of the submerged rocks, until they finally broke through.

"Okay, you ready?"

She nodded emphatically, and he took her hands and placed them in the positions where his hands had been. He might have removed his hands but not his body. A little beside her, a little behind her, he guided her every move. His close presence brought back the butterflies again, but soon her task at hand overcame them.

After a few minutes of puttering, Lydia got the hang of manning the vessel and opened her up. She screeched at the power the fast pace gave her. Exhilarating didn't come close to describing the freeing feeling. Her screeches turned to all-out laughter.

She never heard Wesley laugh, but when she peered out the sides of her eyes she found his smile locked on her.

As well as the dented eyebrows of puzzlement. Something confused him.

She raised her own eyebrows at him to ask what, but he changed his attention forward. "So, do I pass the driver's test?" she asked.

Wesley didn't answer.

Lydia thought maybe he hadn't heard her over the engine noise. She repeated herself.

"Hold on, Doc," he said, taking over the wheel. "There's an unknown vessel out at sea a little too close to my liking. Might be someone off course."

Lydia moved back and scanned the horizon. At first she didn't see what he was talking about. Then a speck of something white appeared way off in the distance. "Is it a boat?"

"A yacht."

"You don't know who they are?"

"We're going to find out."

He shifted the boat into high speed, buckling Lydia's knees. Her hands shot out for the bench seat behind her before she fell to the floor. "A little warning next time, please." She put a little bite into her words as she took her seat.

"I'll try to remember." He didn't sound too convincing.

Wesley skimmed across the ocean until they finally pulled up to the yacht's portside and turned off the motor. He lifted a bullhorn to his mouth. "This is the sheriff of Stepping Stones. I need the captain of the vessel to please step out on deck."

No sound but the waves lapping the hulls below and the seagulls squeaking above in the sunshine could be heard.

"You have thirty seconds to come out or I come aboard," Wesley warned through the megaphone, but still no reply came.

Lydia offered her two cents. "I don't think anyone's here. It's too quiet."

"I agree," he replied, his voice deep and serious. His hand went to his belt to flip the holster cover off his gun. "Wait here. I'm going aboard." Leaning over he pulled his boat closer to make the leap across to the aft of the yacht. His body moved in a perfect blend of fluidity and muscled strength.

She watched him slink around the side of the yacht and up the stairs to the pilothouse with its black-tinted windows. He disappeared through a portal as though its dark shadows swallowed him whole.

Minutes went by with Lydia turning an ear for Wesley's or anyone's drifting voice. The small police boat rocked in the swells, up and down, lulling her senses until she realized a lot of time had passed. Going aboard didn't feel like an option and was way out of her expertise, unless someone was dead *and* decomposed.

She checked her watch and drank her coffee but couldn't shake her gut feeling that trouble brewed out on the high seas.

* * *

Wesley held his gun as he traversed through the rooms of the ninety-foot luxurious Expeditions yacht. The place was beyond anything he'd ever been in or imagined. He knew there were people out there who lived in the lap of luxury—he knew of some—but that didn't make this experience any less eye-opening.

He passed through the dining room, the table set with gold utensils. *Gold, seriously? Does it make the food taste any better?* His head swiveled and met the golden statue head of an Egyptian princess sitting on an ivory carved pedestal. He peered closer. They both looked pretty old. In fact, as he roamed through the room and down the hall into the last great room, everywhere his eyes landed, he gawked at ancient art in one form or another.

Either whoever owned this vessel had spent their lifetime collecting antiquities or Wesley had happened upon an art thief's black-market pillages. Perhaps they were modern-day pirates seeking to hide their stash on these shores again. Wes snickered at the idea but secretly wished that was the case. He knew he wouldn't like the real reason this boat was near his island.

Especially since its owner was missing.

Wes had covered every square foot of the layout and had come across no one. The yacht was empty except for its expensive contents.

He scanned the large and final room. Past a bar and leather furniture. Past a pool table with a game half played, the black eight ball eyeing him from the center of the table. The largest flat-screen television he'd ever seen hung from the back wall, a closed metal door a few feet to its right.

One more room to explore. Judging by the metal door, he figured this was the engine room. Wes kept his gun ready as he approached the door. A twist and pull swung it wide. The room gleamed spotless...and empty. The engine was closed off behind a metal gate. A clean stainless-steel counter with drawers below shone. A tall steel locker cabinet stood cornered in the small room.

Tall enough to fit a person.

As Wes approached with careful steps, the

door behind him swung closed on a bang. He shot around to no one. Automatic hinges. He crossed the floor, his boots light and silent. Another twist and the metal doors clanged open to empty hooks.

Nothing and nobody. This vessel was unmanned.

He headed for the exit, but a last gaze around the room halted on a black duffel bag sitting on a shelf. Curiosity had him moving in. Maybe there would be something identifying in the bag.

The top flap was unzipped, partially open. A quick flick lifted it up. Wes's stomach dropped to his knees at the sight of the bag's contents.

A bomb!

The homemade contraption had a tangle of colorful wires connecting one small black box to a liquid explosive in a clear container. The red digital numbers counting down halted his inspection and hope of disabling it. If his eyes were reading the dropping digits correctly, they told him he had less than two minutes to get off this boat. No time to fool around with wires.

Wes made a dash for the metal door, his hand outstretched for the doorknob before his feet could reach. A twist and pull did nothing. *Dear God, no! I can't be locked in here.* He yanked harder and harder. Sweat broke out on his forehead. His hand slipped off the doorknob, also slick with sweat.

A minute five and counting.

Wes contemplated yanking all the wires out but knew that could detonate the bomb immediately. His hand fisted and relaxed, fisted and relaxed as he came to the acceptance that he was locked in here with no hope of an escape.

Thirty seconds.

He looked around the room. The metal locker was his only choice. He made a mad dash for the container with five seconds remaining.

A loud, muffled bang from the boat's interior jolted Lydia to her feet, and then down to the boat's deck. Coffee sloshed all over her before the cup rolled away, forgotten.

Lydia twisted around, pushing herself up

on her knees to find black smoke drifting up into the atmosphere, coming from the other side of the yacht.

Questions ran through her mind. What was that bang? Is that a fire making the smoke?

Is Wesley alive?

Lydia jumped to her feet in the same moment the two-way radio on Wesley's boat chirped. "Wes, do you read?"

Lydia's lips grew pained from her teeth biting into them. She stood on her tiptoes, squinting to see through the tinted pilothouse's windows. Where was Wesley? Had he been hurt in whatever that bang was?

"Wes, this is Owen. Do you read?"

Lydia stepped to the side of the boat. She kept her eyes on the handheld radio still chirping, and shot her hand out for it, finding the button on the side. "Owen? This is Lydia. Wesley went aboard a yacht in the ocean and there was some sort of bang, and now there's a fire on the other side of the hull. He hasn't come back out. I'm not sure what to do."

"Where are you?"

"I don't know." She searched the land to

give a frame of reference. "I see the ferry dock from here, but it's pretty far. I see a big red boathouse straight ahead on the island. At least I think that's what it is. It's pretty substantial. Looks like it holds a lot of boats."

"Hang on. I know where you are. I see the smoke now."

Lydia climbed up on the side to try and get a better view inside the yacht. A few steps later, and her feet hit the vessel's deck.

She halted. Should she go any farther? *Father, I know what I heard was an explosion. If someone is hurt, then that is something I can help with. Please stay with me, though.* Lydia ran toward the stairs as Wesley had done and reached the top. She peered in.

Empty.

"Wesley?" she called out again, her voice squeaky like the seagulls. She swallowed hard and called again.

A door at the back of the pilothouse was closed. Lydia stepped up to it, placing her hand on the cold metal latch. She froze in indecision. After a few deep breaths, she opened it toward her and a cloud of smoke hit her in the face. She waved her hand to peer through and found a dark, steep staircase going down to the bottom floor. She took the steps while she listened intently.

No sound of people could be heard ahead, just what sounded like the crackle of fire.

"Wesley? It's me, Lydia. Are you down here?" she yelled at the last step, standing on the outskirts of a large room filled with flames and smoke.

"Go…back!" A muffled voice grabbed her attention from somewhere close by.

It was Wesley. She was sure of it. Even faint as it was, she knew. She also knew he sounded distressed. Was he hurt or blocked in behind the fire? She couldn't leave him. But where was he? She could barely see her hand in front of her face. How would she find him in here and in time?

Lydia headed to her right and found a wall. Her hand felt along a few steps. "Hang on, Wesley! I'm coming!"

"No! Lydia, get off the boat! Now!" The voice came from her left. She whipped around to find where he called from. Somewhere on the far side of the room. "I'm coming!"

Her hands went up in front of her to feel her way across the room.

As she stepped out, debris tripped her up. She fell to the floor but kept crawling. A little easier to breathe down near the floor, she crawled forward, but her throat burned from the smoke. Her lungs ached and her eyes burned. She told her body to move, to find Wesley, who was in this room somewhere. He could be hurt. He might need help. She forced her eyes to open and felt heat dry the surface of her eyes as she realized fire lapped directly in front of her. She tried to turn back but couldn't go anywhere.

Two flaming tongues blocked her in. She'd come to a dead end.

Just beyond the flames, she could hear Wesley banging on something. A door? He was blocked in, too. All she wanted was to help him, but with the barrier of scorching heat between them and around them, she could do nothing for him now.

Or herself.

The flames pressed in, searing her lungs with each of her breaths and leaving little doubt that helping Wesley might have been a bad decision on her part.

Wesley kicked and kicked, trying to get out of the cabinet. The explosion had dented it, making its hinges unmovable. After many attempts, the door gave way to a smoke-and fire-filled engine room. As hard as getting out was, the cabinet saved his life, and judging by the fact that he was still alive, the bomb hadn't done what it was supposed to do. It must have malfunctioned...not that he was complaining.

He ignored the pain in the shoulder that had taken the brunt of the impact and the ringing in his ears. He checked the doorway and saw the door had blown off.

He was free—except for the fire blocking his path.

Glad for his fireproofed uniform coat, Wesley hiked it up over his face and began to dodge and weave through the growing flames. The engine could still catch fire and blow the whole boat sky-high, but he wanted to be long gone by then.

Without waiting for three, he went up and over the flickering flames that were blocking the threshold of the room. He landed in a run with balls of fire as obstacles. He still had to get through the lounge, and with the smoke filling the room up, he couldn't see past the flame in front of him. Weaving left to right, he hurdled over the dangerous bellows one by one until he reached the bottom of the stairs.

When his foot hit the first tread, a cough sounded from behind.

Wesley swung back around to the smoke-filled room. Someone was down here and in the flames. Was it Lydia? Had she stayed down after he told her to leave? Was she in the flames somewhere?

Wesley confronted the inferno again. It crept close to his feet. He wondered how long they had before the whole boat erupted. "Lydia!" he called out, and stepped straight a few paces. "Lydia, are you in here?"

"Wesley?" a faint voice came from the wall with the bar, followed by more fits of coughing.

She had to be on the floor. "Hang on, Doc. I'm coming!" Thoughts for his welfare vanished. He let his mind rationalize that this fact was because someone was hurt on his watch, but somewhere deep inside he knew he never felt such a rising panic over any of his islanders before.

Regardless of why he felt this different response, and regardless of the heat charring his eyebrows, he pressed in farther. Step by step, intense temperatures pushed at him as he pushed through. He edged around each whipping flame, jumping a few that were birthed from other flames. Sweat trickled down the searing flesh of his neck. Smoke clouded his vision and filled his lungs. He hit the edge of the bar and knocked the noxious fumes out in a rush.

"Lydia!" he choked.

"Here!" she answered, her voice close but muffled. "Behind…bar."

Wesley grabbed the lip of the bar and let it guide him around to the back. The next moment, his foot met her leg, and he dropped to the floor.

The air was a little clearer down here. He could make out her shape and position. She lay curled up in the fetal position, pressed into the back of the bar, her face tucked into her chest and arms. He scooped her up and she lifted her chin to meet his gaze. "I tried." She coughed. "To get…to you. But fire—"

"Shh. We'll talk later. We've got to get out of here." He wrapped his arms under her legs to lift her.

"I'll…walk," she said, pushing at his chest.

He ignored her and hefted her up as he stood. "Don't fight me. You're no small pixie, and I could drop you in the flames. Put your face into my coat." With her in his arms, he stepped back into the thick of the smoke. As he instructed, she plastered her face into the crook of his arm while he shielded her long frame as much as he could with his thick-coated sleeve. "Hang on!" he yelled as he made his first sidestep around a hot orange flare.

The door loomed ahead in the black haze.

Wesley put his face into his shoulder to take another breath before attempting a leap over the lower of the two flames in front of him. Sharp needles of pain cut his lungs as he landed closer to the exit. He picked up his pace as he stepped forward, nearly free and clear—until a blast roared up in his path too fast for him to avoid.

"My arm!" Lydia cried out.

The sleeve of her parka ignited in fire. The flaring sight knocked the tight air from his chest, but the only thing he could do at the moment was push through. One more leap had him colliding with the wall and depositing her on her feet in the same moment.

She fumbled with the zipper, her hands a trembling mess. His weren't much better, but he managed to push hers aside to make a clean escape. He ripped her jacket from her back, tossing it to the floor, and grabbed her arm to find her sweater charred through.

"Come on!" Wesley pulled her up the stairs behind him. They just had to get out the door at the top before the boat blew.

Most boats had fire suppression systems in

the engine room to extinguish a fire in the engine so it wouldn't blow, but would that include an all-out blaze like this? And if the person who set the bomb wanted the boat to explode, he might have shut the suppression system down. He remembered her arm and yanked her blackened sleeve up. "How's your arm?" he asked, his voice scratchy and raw. An edge of anger he couldn't control layered in it as well. He felt more of that chest-tightening panic from before as he inspected the frayed and burned clothing.

"It's okay," she rasped. "I think my flame-retardant thermals staved off the burn all the way through."

He should have been relieved, but his pumping adrenaline wouldn't let his fight mode relent. His emotions still felt raw, and so did his words. "Thermals? I'm surprised you planned enough to remember any warm clothes at all." He pulled her farther up the stairs with him, knowing he pulled her too hard, but only because he fought against the need to pull her into his arms which was what he really wanted to do.

"Why are you so mad?" she asked from behind.

"I told you to get off this boat. What were you doing in there?" He tossed his chin in the direction behind them as they trudged farther up the stairs.

"I couldn't just leave you in there," she shot at his back.

"It's not your job to protect me." He reached the last two steps and made a grab for the doorknob.

It didn't budge.

"So sorry," she said, oblivious of the danger they were back in again. "Whoever was supposed to protect you wasn't available."

Wesley went for his gun at his belt but came up empty. Shock made way to remembrance. He'd dropped it in his mad dash for the locker.

Panic set in. They were locked inside a stairwell with a fire creeping up behind them, and he had no way of getting Lydia to safety. His only recourse was to kick the door as he had the locker. He lifted a leg in front of him and jammed it right below the doorknob.

His body vibrated, but not the door. "There is no one to protect me—" he kicked "—or miss me—" his shoulder jammed "—or otherwise." His breaths gained momentum while he leaned against the door for a quick break. *This thing must be made of oak,* he thought. "I can't say the same for you."

"What are you doing?" she cried in a moment of confusion. "Are we locked in?"

"You're brilliant, Doc." He swiped the sweat from his forehead. He noticed a wisp of smoke floated passed at eye level. He looked down past Lydia to see bright orange tongues lap up at them as if they searched them out.

In the next instant, Lydia came barreling up beside him, heaving her body into the door. He joined her, and the two of them put every ounce of effort they had into breaking it down. Twice. Twice more. Another heave. Another kick. Exhaustion showed on Lydia's face, but she didn't relent. At first her heaves were accompanied by a good black belt's kiai. Then her voice faded along with her gusto until she stopped her pushing completely.

Wesley pushed on, heaving his shoulder

into the door three more times before she placed a hand on his forearm. He heaved again while his gaze locked on her slender-boned hand.

"It's over, Wesley."

It's over? He hated those words, and all their various levels of meaning. An image of the last girl who'd said them flashed in his mind.

Wesley pushed it out and focused on Lydia's liquid-brown eyes. She wasn't that girl. She wasn't a liar like Jenny. The dancing flames reflecting in her glasses proved it. The fire was here to claim them. Her words rang true.

It was over.

The two of them leaned as far away from the rising scorches as they could. Their bodies plastered against the door, their faces inches apart.

"I'm sorry." His voice was coarse and scratched from the smoke.

"Nothing to forgive." Her lips trembled while she squeezed his arm in restrained fear.

He couldn't accept what she was offering

him. "I was supposed to protect you. You're on my island, and I failed you."

She shook her head. A long tendril of silky hair escaped her tight bun and fell to the side of her stoic face. She faced death with no hysteria. Her fear checked. Nothing out of control but her hair.

Her hair.

Wes grabbed at the sides of her head. He threaded frantically into the sides and back of her silky hair.

"What are you doing?" she demanded.

"Looking for a pin. Do you have any in here?" He continued to grapple at this last attempt to save her.

"A pin? A pin! Yes, I have a pin in here somewhere. Her hands reached up, brushing against his. Their fingers tangled together before she found what they were searching for. A pin keeping her hair pulled back.

She brought the stickpin out and forced it in his hand. "Can you pick the lock?"

"Yes." He got down to his knees, trying to make a connection with the pin and lock mechanisms as fast as possible, but also carefully so as to make that connection on the first try.

"Can you pick it, like, *now?*" The panic in her voice told him the fire was on her. He hated to hear her whimper and used that to push him.

"Almost…*there!*" Wes turned the knob and pushed the door wide. He reached around her waist and threw her out the door ahead of him. Together they fell forward in a scrambling heap away from the door.

He lifted his head to look over Lydia's. She coughed in fits, but his eyes locked only on a pair of men's brown boots belonging to someone who stood over them.

Had the yacht owner come home? Wesley pushed Lydia to his left and pooled the last of his resources. After fighting a battle of flames, he still had one more battle to fight.

THREE

Pain slammed into Lydia's lungs with each wrenching cough. One hand covered her mouth while the other reached for Wesley. He'd pushed her to the side, and she didn't understand why. She noticed he looked up above her.

Someone stood there.

She craned her neck and raised her eyes higher and higher until she recognized Owen, his mouth moving in what seemed like soundless shouts. Slowly his words became clear and focused as Lydia realized he yelled for them to keep moving. She whipped her head downward to see the flames protruding out the doorway. In the next instant, Wesley lifted her under her armpits and dragged her across the floor. In a muffled daze, she was pulled away from the fiery place she'd stood moments before.

Lydia's mind snapped to attention. She cranked her neck up and saw Wesley yelling at her. Owen stepped up to her side, his mouth moving with muffled sounds.

"…you hurt?" The last words of his sentence phased in loud and clear.

Lydia shook her head, but wasn't really sure of anything at the moment.

Now that the roar of the fire and the roar in her head quieted, the outside world came alive again. And she realized so was she.

A new rush of adrenaline pushed her to retreat. Or perhaps that was Wesley. She could feel his hands on her back, guiding her with some force out the door and down the side stairs to where their boat was tied to the yacht.

He came up beside her and jumped across first, then turned with arms out to help her vault over. He deposited her on the seat and turned back to untie the ropes. "Owen! Find out who owns this yacht before there's nothing left to it."

"I'm already on it!" he called back from his own boat.

"I'm taking Lydia to the clinic. I'll meet you over at the site." Wesley put the boat in reverse and zipped back, but before pulling out, he called out, "Hey, Owen! If you're here, then who's watching the skeleton?"

Owen hesitated. He swung his head around in the direction of the burial site. His lack of an answer told them all the remains were unguarded.

Another of her gut feelings twisted her stomach. Lydia rushed to the wheel and croaked out, "Wesley, forget the clinic. Get over to the site…now." She grabbed her aching throat. "I think this was a setup."

His jaw ticked as a look of anger crossed his face. "Here's the warning you asked for earlier, Doc. You might want to have a seat. We're about to go real fast. If the fire was a decoy, someone is going to pay. And not just for tricking me, but for putting your life at risk."

Wesley propelled his boat across the sea at breakneck speed. He had to concur with Lydia's opinion of the yacht fire being a setup.

And he fell for it.

Why hadn't he seen it? It wasn't as if this was the first time he fell for someone's ploys. But this time was different. This time Lydia nearly paid for it with her life.

Wes pushed through the waves, circling the island toward the secluded, craggy side. Rough rocks began to jut up out of the sea. He brought the throttle down to a safe but still fast speed while navigating in and around them.

Up ahead, he sought the direction of the burial site for movement, but saw nothing but the high mounds of sand and wispy brown grasses blocking his view of the skeleton that hopefully still lay beyond them.

A flat rock near shore would be a good place to drop anchor. Normally, he would have extended the portable dock for Lydia, but she didn't look as though she wanted to wait any more than he did.

She gripped the side of the boat, waiting for his call to make the jump. At his nod, she vaulted over the side and landed smoothly on the rock and took off running. Sand and pebbles lifted in her wake. He kept right up with her until they came over the hill.

Wesley's feet halted, but Lydia kept on running, skidding to a stop at the remains.

The skeleton lay at rest. Nothing looked disturbed in the already disturbing scene, except for one major thing.

The skull was gone.

Nothing but heaps of overturned sand gave witness that it had been there at all. If it hadn't been a crime scene before, it definitely was one now. "Lydia, I need you to come out of there."

She looked up at him, staggered and silent.

"I need you to come back up here before the land is too disturbed to trace any shoeprints."

Lydia backtracked, carefully placing her shoes in her own prints. She turned dismayed eyes on him. "Now what?"

"Now we figure out who didn't want her found."

"How?"

"As you said yesterday, there might be other items like clothing in there that might give us a clue to her identity, or the identity of who buried her."

"Right." Lydia looked to where the boat was anchored. "Plus, I did take a few pictures, not that I can make a cast from a photo, but I might be able to use the photo as an ID *if* we find her again."

"Then it's a plan." He studied her profile for a few beats. She grabbed her throat where he knew it burned from the smoke inhalation. The black charred mark on the arm of her white sweater gave proof to the danger around them. "Unless you would rather bail after that fire. It's pretty obvious someone doesn't want the skeleton identified if they're willing to cause such an expensive and dangerous diversion."

"And they have no problem killing again in the process," she replied with her quick and right-on assessment.

"Hey, Wes." Deputy Matthews appeared over the mound. "I got the details of who owns, or owned, I should say, the yacht." Owen's blue eyes shot a nervous glance in Lydia's direction.

"Go ahead, Owen. What are you waiting for?" Wes said without hiding his impatience.

Owen cleared his throat. "Believe it or not, it belongs to Calvin Carmichael. Jenny's father."

Air expelled from Wes's lungs, leaving him unable to respond. His mind practically exploded as the bomb had.

Lydia's chin tilted. "I don't understand. Who's Calvin Carmichael?" She faced Owen when Wes failed to reengage. "Who's Jenny?"

Owen's dark brown eyebrows rose. "Do you want to tell her, or do you want me to?"

Wes barely heard them over his own mind-blaring questions. He scanned the sea as though the billows of smoke reaching sky-high had the answers. If that was Calvin Carmichael's yacht, did that mean Jenny was here?

No. She'd said she'd never return. *It's over,* her letter had said.

"Wes?" Owen's voice pulled him back to his job. "Do you want to tell her?"

Wesley trailed his fingers through his hair, letting the strands fall wherever they wanted, and answered Lydia's question. "Jenny was my fiancée."

"Oh." Surprise marred Lydia's face. "I didn't realize. I'm sorry to hear that. What happened? If you don't mind me asking."

"Simple. She left me." Wes swallowed hard. "On a big expensive yacht like the one burning to a crisp. She didn't want to slum it with me and set her sights on someone richer. He came and picked her up and she never looked back."

Lydia squinted past his shoulder toward the drifting smoke. "Do you think she's come back?"

"There's only one way to find out." Wes shook his head. "I vowed I'd never do this, but it looks like I have no choice. I'm going to have to call her."

Wes held his phone in his hand, unable to hit Call. It shouldn't be this hard. After five years, he accepted Jenny's split was the best thing to ever happen to him. She'd left him with nothing but a cutting Dear-John letter in the wake of her new man's yacht.

Wes pushed a pile of newspapers off his couch and onto the floor to make room to sit. Sitting might make this call easier. But still his thumb hovered over the call button. His leg bounced as he rubbed a sweaty palm down the thigh of his blue jeans. He jumped to his feet. Walking would be better after all.

He beat a path in the orange shag carpet toward the breakfast counter. It divided his galley kitchen from the living/dining room.

What dining room? You don't own a dining room.

Not to the likes Jenny had grown up with. She always said it didn't matter.

Until her letter said it did.

She was a Carmichael. Deep down Wes had known eventually money would call her back. But a naïve part of him had hoped maybe, just maybe, his love and the simple life he offered her on the island would be enough for her. That *he* would be enough for her. And that she would be what he needed to heal his aching heart.

The death of his parents had changed him. Especially the death of his mother. The ache it left in him was more than grief. He didn't know what it was. All he knew was when he thought of Sarah Grant, he felt like throwing something. Maybe it would have been different if he'd been here when she died. If he had a chance to say goodbye. If only she told him to come home. But she hadn't, and all he could think was she thought he cared more about his career than her?

For all the Proverbs his mother recited, she was a foolish woman if that was the case.

Soon after her death, he lost his job at the art museum in Boston and had to come back to Stepping Stones anyway. The islanders welcomed him and believed in him as if he were family, and Wesley realized they were the closest thing to family he would ever have. He vowed to serve and protect them and this land from then on.

Then Jenny showed up on the Sunday ferry and life got even better. She said she was choosing him over her rich family. And he believed in her enough to put a ring on her finger.

Now who was the fool?

He hit Call.

Four rings. Five. Six. He didn't know what he would even say if she answered. He should try tomorrow after he planned this better.

No. He'd already held off all day. Another day couldn't go by. Not when Lydia nearly died today. This couldn't wait. As soon as someone answered, he would get to the bottom of this, then hang up.

Seven. Eight.

"Hello?" a woman answered. Was it Jenny? The voice sounded like hers. Wesley's stomach knotted and he was glad he'd skipped dinner.

"Hello, is this Jennifer Carmichael?"

Silence.

"Hello?" Wes repeated.

"Who is this?" the woman whispered harshly.

"This is Sheriff Grant of Stepping Stones Island." He breathed deep and pushed out the inevitable question. "Who is this?"

"Hold on a minute." The phone clanged to a hard surface. Minutes passed. Wesley had begun to think the woman wasn't coming back until he could hear yelling in the background. A man's voice this time. Footsteps beat out a cadence and got louder until the phone was picked back up.

"Sheriff Grant." A man spoke this time. "You wouldn't happen to be Wesley Grant, would you?"

"Yes, I'm Wesley Grant. I was engaged to Jennifer."

"Now, you listen here. I don't want any problems from you."

"I'm not calling to cause problems. It's for police matters, and actually, if this is Calvin Carmichael, I need to ask you a few questions."

Silence again.

"Mr. Carmichael?" Wesley could only assume it was Carmichael on the other end.

"Jennifer's dead."

"Ex— Excuse me?" Wesley's voice bounced around his cranium like a twisted game of Ping-Pong. He hadn't been expecting that response.

Jenny was dead?

"She drowned off the coast of Malta five

years ago," Mr. Carmichael informed him in a low tone as though he didn't speak on the matter often.

"Five years ago! How? Wait, why didn't you contact me?" Wesley's breathing picked up, matching the pace of his feet as they moved him across the room a few times.

"Jennifer made her decision to cut you out of her life when she left you. We honored her wishes."

"Her wishes?" Wesley balked, then sighed as Mr. Carmichael's words penetrated his thick skull and made full sense. "Right. Her wishes."

"She was very happy, Mr. Grant. Her husband gave her the world. We take comfort knowing her last days were spent with the man she loved."

Wes ignored the jab and wrapped his brain around the fact that his Jenny was dead. No, not *his* Jenny. Someone else's Jenny. Her husband made her happy. He gave her the world.

I couldn't even give her a dining room.

Wes swallowed this fact to focus on the investigation at hand. "I'm sorry for your loss,

Mr. Carmichael, but right now I need to ask you about your yacht."

"You know where my yacht is?" The question came swift and accusatory.

"As a matter of fact, I do. It's in my bay, burned to a crisp. I was hoping you could tell me why."

"Burned?" the man yelled through the phone. "Why would they do that—" He halted.

"Who is this *they* you speak of?" Wesley asked.

"No one. I don't know. The people who stole it out of the marina two days ago. I can't believe—"

"Did you file a police report?"

"Of course I filed a report. You can check with the Boston police if you feel that is necessary."

"Thank you, sir, I will."

"I need to go."

"Wait!" Wes tried to catch the man before he hung up in his obvious haste.

"What now?"

"I just need to know. For no other reason but just to know." Wes paused. "Where is

Jenny buried?" The acceptance Wes heard in his voice surprised him. After the initial shock of the news of Jenny's death, indifference set in. At one time, this news would have crippled him.

Mr. Carmichael breathed heavy; his sigh of confliction came through the phone lines. "You can find her stone in Boston. Near Harvard."

Harvard. The place they'd met. She a grad student, he an on-campus police officer. He thought of the first time he saw her that late night sitting on the bench under the lamplight. Her skittish eyes incited a need in him to protect her from that day on. In return, she'd offered him comfort when he shared about his grief over the loss of his parents. She may have chosen the rich life over him, but in the beginning, she really had helped him in his grief.

The least he could do was the same for Calvin Carmichael. "I'm sorry," Wes said while he sorted through the flashes of his memories of her.

"Well, you should be," Mr. Carmichael

blurted back, jolting Wesley back to the present. "We lost our daughter and missed out on the last year of her life because of you. It's only because of the happiness her husband gave her that I can stand here today and speak civilly to you. But don't expect this again. What I want to know is how are you still working in law enforcement when you're nothing but a thief?"

Wesley's anger buoyed up from its regular resting place—right below the surface. "I was innocent. I never stole anything from your museum, and you know it."

"The only thing I know is you belong behind bars, not wearing an officer of the law's uniform. Apparently, you've fooled your town like you fooled my daughter." The phone went dead. Carmichael had hung up. Wes tossed his phone behind him somewhere and headed for his back door. Cooling off felt like a must at the moment.

He stepped out onto the back porch of his small clapboard cottage and crunched down the crushed-seashell walkway to the shoreline. The crash of waves echoed through the bitter-cold night air. He breathed deeply of the harsh temp, welcoming tiny shards of ice into his lungs. He clomped out onto the wooden dock and breathed again, willing the cold to numb his anger from the inside.

Fooled his daughter? The man was way off. It was *Jenny* who did the fooling. It was Jenny who did the lying. It was Jenny who did the cheating.

It was Jenny who did the leaving.

The only thing Wesley was guilty of was trusting her enough to put a ring on her finger. He would never make that mistake again.

FOUR

"Do you need any help?"

Lydia searched over her shoulder for the feminine voice drifting down from the top of the sand mound. Pat Reed's hazel-eyed stare waited expectantly for an answer to her offer. Her crazy, frazzled red hair whipped in the wind to her right, directly into Deputy Vaughn's face.

"No, thank you." Lydia gained her feet before the two people brought any of their DNA to the scene. It was hard enough collecting minute trace evidence that might prove someone had been on the scene, never mind introducing more for her to collect. She dusted the sand from the knees of her white coveralls and stepped forward to act as a human barrier. "Pat, you shouldn't be here. If I find even one strand of your hair, I'll have to include in my report that it was found on the scene. That would make you a suspect."

"Seriously?" Pat touched her unruly hair, tucking it behind her ear to unsuccessfully tame it down. She brought the hood of her red down jacket up to cover her head. "There. How's that?"

"You still shouldn't be here."

"I just want to help. Your job is so fascinating. Can't I just watch?"

Lydia sent a pleading look in the portly deputy's direction. "Perhaps Deputy Vaughn needs help putting the tent up."

"No, ma'am, I can handle that on my own, but thank you." He left them for the rolled-up tent that lay in the sand. So much for the man catching her drift.

"Okay, fine, you can watch, but stay where you are. Don't come down off that mound."

"Got it."

Lydia knelt back in the spot she'd been working in. She picked up her brush and dusted off a button she'd found before Pat arrived. It matched one she had found earlier and was most likely part of the outfit the victim had been wearing. She would try to find the fashion line it belonged to, and then, hopefully, the outfit it had once been attached to. Knowing what a victim had been wearing the moment he or she went missing could help narrow down the missing persons list.

She dropped it in an evidence bag and labeled it.

"What are you going to do with that?" Pat asked.

"Not me. The investigators. They might be able to track where the outfit had been purchased and when."

"Really? You mean our clothes can give us away?"

"Give you away? That's an interesting way of putting it, but yes." Lydia thought Pat's thinking sounded a little backward, but shrugged it off for sifting through more sand around the left-handed phalanges. She'd hoped for an engagement ring on the third phalange, but came up literally empty-handed. A unique ring could have been a clear indicator of the identity of the woman.

Something a witness could recognize as belonging only to the victim.

"What are you looking for?" Pat interrupted.

"A ring."

"Why?"

Lydia continued to sift while she gave the answer to Pat's question.

"I see," Pat replied, then quickly asked, "Do you know if Wes will be here today? I thought I would see him."

Lydia eyed the woman through the top of her glasses. She realized now why Pat was here, and it had nothing to do with her finding anthropology fascinating. "I have no idea what the sheriff's plans are. He didn't share them with me."

"Yeah, he's like that. Kind of keeps to himself. Ever since *Jenny*." Pat smeared the woman's name like fish pate on a cracker.

A love triangle, it would seem, but Lydia sifted on, her head down. She had no desire to encourage Pat in her slander of Wesley's fiancée. Someone should tell Pat, though, if she had interest in Wesley, defaming the woman he pledged to marry would not endear her to him. It would only be a constant reminder of his failed relationship. If Pat hoped to win Wesley's heart, that wasn't the way to do it.

But then, what did Lydia know about relationships? Maybe Pat was exactly what Wesley wanted.

"He never used to be so serious," Pat continued in her one-sided conversation. "I've known him my whole life. I remember how he used to be so quick with a joke. He always made me laugh, and I didn't even mind him calling me Red."

Lydia could hear the smile in Pat's voice as she went on and on about Wesley. It was obvious Pat had longtime feelings for him that ran deep. Lydia wondered how Wesley could have missed them. He was an observant man. He had to know how Pat felt. Maybe he needed to keep things platonic because of his job. Maybe he really did share Pat's feelings.

Lydia slipped in her digging and nicked the tiniest phalange. She hissed at her carelessness and told herself to focus on her job and less on whose doorstep Wesley laid his heart. It was none of her concern. "It's none of my concern," she said out loud to reaffirm it to herself.

"That's what everyone said," Pat said with more disgust. "It's none of my concern. But how could I not say something? Jenny treated Wesley horribly. I had to do something. I couldn't just stand by and watch her cut him down with her sharp, spoiled tongue. So what if she came from money in Boston? That didn't make her better than Wesley. Better than me!"

A shadow emerged over the skeleton. Pat breached the barrier. She now hovered over her. "Pat—" Lydia warned.

"Patty. My name is Patty. Wesley calls me Pat so he can avoid the fact that I'm a woman. Not some kid down the street anymore."

"Fine, *Patty,* I told you to stay on the mound. Please step back or you'll have to leave."

"Wesley deserved better. He deserved a woman that loved him for himself. Jenny was the one not worthy of him. I still remember the day she showed up here on the ferry, saying she was giving up her fancy life for him. It was right after Wesley lost his campus police job and returned home. Those snobby people tried to put him in jail for a crime he didn't commit. I'd never seen Wesley so mad and hurt. His dreams of a career in law enforcement ended because of Jenny's family. I tried to make him happy, to smile again, but that didn't happen until *she* showed up and told him she loved him."

Patty grunted. "But she lied. Instead of loving him, she destroyed him even more. She left him broken and…different. Now he's so hard and distrustful. All because of her!"

Patty's foot kicked out and made contact with one side of the skeleton's ribs. The lower sections dislodged from their resting place. Lydia threw herself between the skeleton and Patty before more damage could be done.

Appalled, she raised her head and noticed Patty ready to kick again. "Patty! What are you doing?"

Patty snapped out of her rage, her chest heaving in her quick breaths. "I'm sorry. You just don't understand. I miss him. I miss the way he used to be. Before he changed."

"You need to go home now." Lydia pushed up to search for Deputy Vaughn. "Derek! I need your help." The deputy came over the mound. "Please take Patty home. I need to work alone. I work better alone."

Deputy Vaughn reached a hand out for Patty's upper arm. "Is everything all right, Dr. Muir?" He pulled Patty's arm, but she didn't budge.

"Just take her back. Please." Lydia's words fumbled from her mouth as she righted the bones back into their place.

Deputy Vaughn tugged on Patty's arm. "Let's go, Pat. I'll take you home or anywhere else you want to go, but you can't stay here."

"I'm sorry," Patty repeated in a rush as she was led away from the site. "It won't happen again. I just got upset for a second. The whole injustice of it all makes me so angry. Wesley deserved better than her. His mother would be so sad if she saw him now."

Pat's excuses mixed with the sounds of the sea, but her words conjured up images in Lydia's mind that depicted a brokenhearted

Wesley—and provided a possible reason for his bulldog ways.

Lydia scooped sand around to situate the ribs in their proper places. A speck of red caught her eye and paused her digging.

Blood?

That didn't make sense. Skeletons didn't bleed.

She dug out the sand from inside the rib cage, letting it sift through her fingers until the biggest chunk remained in her hand. She grabbed her brush and dusted away the earth from around the object, revealing a rich red color. Bloodred.

But not blood.

A ruby, and a very precious one, judging by its rich color and teardrop cut. This had to be worth a fortune.

Could this gem be the reason this woman died?

But why would the stone still be with her remains? If someone killed her for it, they would have taken it.

Lydia cleaned it off more and grabbed her magnifying glass. Upon closer inspection, she saw tiny holes where the gem had once been attached to a setting of some kind. A ring? She shook her head. The teardrop cut spoke more of a necklace. But where was the rest of it?

She dropped the find into an evidence bag and put it aside. After a thorough dig through the rest of the chest cavity, no more clues appeared. Nothing but the broken-off gemstone to point her in some direction. But direction to where? The chest cavity?

Had the victim swallowed the stone?

Lydia trailed a finger across the nicks and lacerations of some of the ribs. Perhaps the knife wielder knew the stone was inside and tried to retrieve it. Lydia shuddered at the thought.

"What did you find?" a firm, male voice came from behind, causing Lydia's heart to leap into her throat as she swung around.

Wesley.

He stood with one hand at his belt buckle, the other over the gun holstered at his waist. She gulped, her eyes lingering on the gun at her eye level for a beat, then up to his fiercely glittered eyes. He looked madder than she'd seen him yet.

"You scared me. I didn't hear you come in. And I see you replaced your gun."

"For your protection. In fact, because of the bomb, I've decided I don't want you over here by yourself. Now, what did you find?"

Lydia reached for the clear plastic evidence bag with the stone in it. "Grab a pair of gloves and tell me what you think of this." She stood to pass it to him.

"What is it?" he asked while the blue latex slapped tight around his large hands.

Opening the bag, she poured out the stone into his waiting, rubbery palm. "A ruby. A very expensive ruby."

"What, are you a gemologist now, too?"

"No. I just know a good-quality stone when I see one. And that one is pretty rare."

With the stone pinched between his thumb and forefinger, he held it up to the sun. The glint cast a ray of crimson across his face. A face that gave nothing away.

"Well? Do you recognize it?" She stood beside him while he continued to study it.

She heard him grunt and waited for him to elaborate, but nothing came. "Is that a yes?"

His gaze fell to the decapitated skeleton behind her. She pinged a look between him and the remains and back again. If he didn't recognize it, he would have answered by now. "You do recognize it," she stated.

No denial came.

Wesley held out the bloodred jewel to her. "I have to go. I'll radio Matthews to come over so you're not alone." He took off up the mound, sand flying out from under his boots.

"Wait!" Lydia traipsed after him. She reached the top of the mound just as Wesley hit the rocks and jumped into his boat. "Who does this belong to?" she shouted, holding out the gem.

Wesley turned back to her with his hand on the wheel. He looked more confused than she felt. "It belonged to Jenny," he shouted back, and turned the engine over.

She shot a look over her shoulder at the woman's remains.

Jenny? As in the ex-fiancée, Jenny? As in the woman Pat reviled, Jenny?

Am I looking *at Jenny?*

The boat roared away. Lydia whipped back around to see Wesley in an awful hurry, getting smaller and smaller with the distance he quickly put between them.

If this was Jenny lying in the grave, then there were plenty of islanders who would have been happy to put her there. Including the one who just took off.

Especially the one who just took off.

Wesley pulled the string overhead and let it go. The light bulb clicked on but barely filled the rafters of his low-ceilinged attic. Hunched over to a third of his height, he shuffled up the narrow center aisle until he came to the box he knew was up here. He knew it was here because he had been the one to tuck it away out of sight.

But never out of mind.

The cardboard flaps lifted with ease from their present tucked in position. Jenny's letter lay folded on the top of the numerous items she'd left behind. Items not worthy enough to make it into her bags.

Wesley lifted the letter, knowing what lay beneath it. The framed photo of them taken shortly after she'd arrived on Stepping Stones. Just one of the items she deemed unworthy to take.

The letter pulled to him again like the thousand times before. It fell open on its own, its fold having lost its bind after so many readings. Jenny's handwriting swept across the paper evenly and neatly. No hesitation could be gleamed from even one letter. She knew what she wanted to say, and she said it.

"It's over."

Her letter explained her reasons for leaving him for another man. All the reasons she had told him didn't matter in the beginning but, in the end, did. Her claim that money—or lack thereof—wouldn't come between them had been an all-out lie. Everything out of her mouth had been a lie—including her love for him, as the words in her letter stated.

I don't love you. I never did.

He let the letter do what it did best. Remind him that he gave her the power to hurt him when he gave her his trust.

He folded the letter until the next time he needed the reminder and put it aside for the real reason he came up here.

The photo.

His gaze targeted the huge silly grin on his face. Nearly six years ago, he wore it because she had chosen him. Wesley remembered how his cheeks hurt with that very grin when he saw her disembarking the ferry. After everything that had happened. His parents' deaths, him losing his job, her family not accepting him, and even trying to put him in jail. Here she was, running into *his* arms and choosing *him*.

But the grin had faded—and long before she wrote the letter.

He would catch her staring out to sea, deep in thought with her hand at her throat, holding the pendant she wore there always. When he asked her about it, she said it was a family heirloom and she missed her family.

Wesley lifted the photo closer to the light. There, at her throat, was a gold band necklace with a bloodred ruby at its center. After she'd left him, he figured it had been from her real love. Another man besides him because there was no way in the world he could ever afford to give her such a piece.

But no matter where it came from, the necklace became a wedge in their relationship, and he hated the thing because she never took it off. Mountains would have been easier to move than separating her from it. It was a constant, everyday reminder that she belonged to another world.

So then how did it end up buried with another woman on his island after Jenny left?

Unless she never made it off the island and that grave of bones was none other than Jenny.

But what about the body buried in Boston?

Wesley didn't know what to think at this point, except that he had to do whatever it took to find out the truth. He dropped the photo and yanked the light bulb chain. Darkness returned as he hit the ladder and grabbed his keys.

He had a certain bone doctor to see about exhuming a body.

Lydia took a deep breath and let it out slowly. She was about to step out of her comfort zone and enter the Underground Küchen Restaurant alone. Through the glass she could see full tables of people here for the dinner hour. *Lord, help me strike up some chitchat so I don't bore the islanders with my geek talk.*

Honestly, though, she wasn't here for chitchat. She needed to find out if this ruby belonged to Jenny. And she needed to speak with the one person who could give her that answer.

Tildy.

As Wesley put it, Tildy was the local "news reporter" and was the person to see to get the whole story. All Lydia wanted was the story on the ruby. She didn't need any other information, especially information about the relationship between Jenny and Wesley. That was none of her business. She ignored the part of her that still wanted the details regardless. Of course that was only because if the skeleton was Jenny, then another investigator would need to be brought in. Wesley would not be able to investigate a case where he was one of the suspects.

Lydia stepped out of the cold, wet air and into the warm, welcoming restaurant with its roaring fire and cheerful conversations going on.

Professionalism always, she told herself and ignored the comforting feeling the place and these people offered.

These people who were also suspects.

"You're back! Welcome!" Tildy's craggy voice yelled over the din. Her bleached-blond hair bounced behind some patrons before Lydia got a clear view of the lady. Her flouncy apron barely covered anything, and Lydia tried to imagine her own stick of a body holding Tildy's garment up correctly. It wasn't anatomically possible.

"Yes, I am. I was hoping for a table, but I can see I should have called ahead."

"Nonsense, I have the perfect place for you. Come, come."

Lydia's hope for a backroom corner spot fizzled. Instead she followed her leader to the center of the restaurant to a jam-packed table. She cleared a few used plates and mugs from a place setting. "Here you go. Best seat in the house. Len, move it," Tildy ordered the man already sitting there.

"Oh, no," Lydia interrupted. "He doesn't have to move. I can—"

"Of course I can move." A smiling old man pushed back from the table and barely made it to his feet. Hunched over, he held the ladder-back chair for Lydia to sit. "My lady." He insinuated for her to take a seat.

"Oh, no, please, I can't take your seat. That wouldn't be right."

"It wouldn't be right for me not to give it up for one such as lovely as you. And please call me Len." He held his smile, anxious for her to oblige him his chivalry. What could she say?

Nothing other than "Okay, Len. Thank you very much." Lydia sat and took in the curious but friendly stares of the locals around her. As isolated as the island was, the people didn't feel isolating.

A few people around the table shifted and another chair was brought in next to her. Lydia relaxed a bit to see Len plant his old, crooked body back down before he fell down.

"I'll be right back with your dinner," Tildy said, and bounced herself toward the kitchen.

"But I didn't see a menu…yet," Lydia called, her voice trailing off when Tildy disappeared through the set of swinging doors.

"Don't you worry, everything Tildy serves is wonderful," Len reassured.

Lydia sat back in her chair. "So I've heard. Sheriff Grant says she's kept him alive."

"That she has. After his parents passed away, she made sure he was well taken care of."

Lydia's chest squeezed tight, but not from anxiety anymore. This ache fell under empathy for someone who had felt twice the pain she went through. "I lost my mom when I was fourteen, but I couldn't imagine losing my dad, too. He's my biggest champion." And her biggest competitor, but she left that part out. "When did Wesley's—I mean Sheriff Grant's—parents die?"

"Oh, I believe he was about twenty-five years old, so I'd say it's been ten years now since Sheriff Grant Senior passed away. Sarah died two years after her husband."

"His dad was the sheriff?"

"That he was." Len sprouted a sudden Maine accent that didn't match his other one.

"All right, I can tell you aren't an original Mainer, so where are you from?"

"Well, there's a reason why you're sitting in a German restaurant off the coast of Maine. Me and a couple of my friends fled East Germany after World War Two. The Soviets came in and began to persecute many people, including us Christians. We weren't allowed to graduate with our class, and when we saw many being imprisoned, we risked our lives for freedom. It was a tough road, or I should say voyage, but we made it across the sea and searched until we found a place we could feel safe and call home."

Lydia leaned in closer, listening to this old man retell his astounding story and reminisce of his early days here on Stepping Stones. The other people at the table remained quiet as they listened, as well. By their smiles, she could tell they'd probably heard the tales a million times, but they still offered this man, who had to be at least ninety years old, the respect he'd earned. Lydia could see why Wesley wanted to protect these people so much.

And also why they might want to protect him from a certain woman who mistreated him.

"Len, I'm fascinated about all you've been through," Lydia said. "Being true to your faith in a world that doesn't always agree or, as in your case, wants to hurt you for it, is commendable. I could learn so much from you. Perhaps someday you can tell me more."

"But not right now," he said.

Lydia smiled as she shook her head. "I wish I was here for pleasure, but I'm not."

"I figured as much. Can I be of assistance?"

Lydia perused the people at the table, then reached into her new coat's pocket and withdrew the bagged ruby. "I found this with the skeleton. I'm assuming it belonged to the victim. I was hoping someone could tell me if they recognized it." She slid it over to him just as a huge plate of knockwurst slammed down in front of her.

"We've never seen it before in our lives," Tildy brusquely answered. All the warmth

Lydia felt when she came in went up the chimney with the smoke.

"Calm down, Tildy. The girl is just doing her job," Len said, and scooped up the clear bag. "Well, well."

"Well, well, nothing. We don't recognize it." Tildy swiped it from Len's hand, then handed it back to Lydia without looking at it. "It's probably left over from the pirates."

"That is possible," Len said. "You see, long before my friends and I found Stepping Stones, some pirates used to use this island as their home base. They left many artifacts behind. They carved out tunnels into the cliffs to hide their loot and to make escape passages. In fact, the back of this restaurant you're in right now has a tunnel that leads straight up to the top of the cliff where my house sits."

"So you think this was left here by pirates?" Lydia asked Len straight. She really didn't think he would lie. Not after his life's trials he just shared about. She didn't think he would lie, but he definitely hesitated. "I should tell you the skeleton out there is not an old pirate but a young woman."

Len eyed Tildy and cleared his throat. He nodded and confirmed her suspicions. "The gem looks familiar."

"That's all." Tildy stopped Len from saying more. "It just looks familiar. It could have belonged to anyone. We can't say for sure."

"True," Lydia agreed cautiously. "But do you remember ever seeing it on a woman named Jenny Carmichael?"

The atmosphere in the restaurant deadened to a silence as thick as the crust of bread on her plate. She'd hit a nerve.

Lydia expected to have all eyes turn to disdain on her, but when she chanced a glance around the room, she saw sadness more than anything else. In fact, most of the people couldn't look at her at all.

"Why does this sadden you?" Lydia directed her question to them all, but raised her eyes to Tildy for an answer. The woman's eyes glistened with unshed tears. She pursed her red-lined lips as though to keep from saying what was on her mind.

"I'll tell you why," came a deep male voice becoming very familiar to Lydia. All the people jolted and shifted in their chairs. When Lydia craned her neck around, she saw Wesley standing by the door. He'd pushed his hair out of his eyes, but his frigid stare icing the room had her wishing he hadn't.

Lydia rose to her feet, forcing her hands to stay by her side. Her fingers clutched the fabric of her wool suit, but she wouldn't let her hands move to her front as they really wanted to. She needed a barrier of protection from the lethal look Wesley's sharp features sent her way.

"Okay, please tell me." She hated how her voice quivered. Would he admit he killed his fiancée right here in front of everyone? And what if he did? The islanders would surely side with him. If they were willing to protect him this long, then she was outnumbered. Her back heated with the stares of a roomful of loyal onlookers. "Why does this gem make them sad?"

"Because they know that stone belonged to Jenny."

"And?"

"And they believe I killed her."

The room broke into chaos. "No! No!" could be heard all around her, especially from Tildy. "We don't believe that. We don't think you could ever kill anyone." She walked over to Wesley and placed her hand on his cheek, shaking her head back and forth.

He removed her hand with a sad smile, all ice gone from his eyes when he looked at her. "You're not a very good liar. But it's okay. I can honestly tell you I didn't kill her, and that skeleton is not her, but..." He paused to shush their sighs of relief. "But she is dead."

A collective gasp roamed through the room followed by a burst of "whys" and "hows."

Wesley raised a hand. "Wait. I spoke to her father last night, and he informed me she drowned in the Mediterranean. Nowhere near here. She's buried in Boston so you all can rest your minds. It's not her."

"Well, if the skeleton's not her, then who is it?" someone from behind Lydia asked. "How did it get her ruby?"

Wesley's blue eyes pierced Lydia again

from across the room. His coldness had ebbed, but he could still hold her captive with his stare. Her throat parched to the point it hurt to swallow.

Wesley's lips moved in a blur and she heard her name mentioned. "Dr. Muir is working really hard to figure out who the victim is. As soon as we know something we will share it with you. The department is working around the clock to keep the island safe, and we will get to the bottom of this. But if you know something, even if you don't think it's important, please talk to me or Dr. Muir. Now is not the time to try to protect someone."

Tildy searched the room in confusion, then turned back to Wesley. "What are you saying? Are you saying one of us killed that woman?"

"No, I'm not saying that at all. We all need to be up front about any knowledge we might have. That's all. Now, I need to speak with Dr. Muir privately." He waved a hand toward the door.

Lydia's feet felt glued down. She wasn't ready to go anywhere with him yet, although he did say the skeleton wasn't Jenny. If that was the case, then Wesley wasn't a suspect and she had nothing to fear from him.

With that in mind, Lydia stepped to the door and out into the cold with him. They walked along the boardwalk in silence and came to the pier. She stopped, but he continued to the railing, his back to her as he braced his hands over the wood, his head bent low in front of him. "What if I'm wrong? What if the skeleton is Jenny?"

"Why do you think it might be?"

"The ruby belongs to her. I know for a fact she wouldn't have let it out of her sight." He turned and faced Lydia straight on. "There's only one way to find out the truth. We need to identify the body."

"I can't prove anything without a skull."

"I'm talking about the body in Boston. We could be there by tomorrow."

"You want to exhume a body?"

He shrugged, his face deadpan. "*If* there is one to exhume. I've been thinking about the words Mr. Carmichael chose when I spoke to him. He said I would find Jenny's stone in Boston. He didn't say anything about her."

"You're going to need more evidence than that to exhume a body. They don't just let you dig those things up, you know."

"Then we'll do a different kind of digging. Get the proof we need to show someone had a reason to hunt Jenny down. For all her selfishness and faults, I always thought she was running from something or someone. The night I met her I saw fear in her eyes, and it wasn't the only time. One night she came running to me, crying someone was following her. I checked it out, but didn't see anyone." He stopped and looked out to sea. "I'm beginning to think she used me in more ways than one."

"How did she use you? Can you elaborate?"

His mouth opened and closed a few times before he tightened his lips shut. The tic appeared again in his jaw, and his chin dropped to his chest. He turned back and folded his arms at his chest. In defiance? He could very well be covering up his part in Jenny's death.

But something didn't feel right. Dr. Webber

would chastise her for basing her finding on her feelings instead of evidence, but the more she watched Wesley, the more she thought she recognized hurt and embarrassment in him, not guilt.

A flush spread across his clenched cheeks. Could be residual anger toward Jenny, but the shuffling of his feet said he experienced discomfort in having to open up and tell how Jenny shamed him.

Suddenly, the hair made sense.

Wesley walked around this island full of people who knew what Jenny did to him. The hair kept him from having to see their looks of pity at every encounter. And it probably allowed him to stand taller and do his job with dignity.

Lydia curled her fingers tightly into her palm to stop them from brushing the silky blond strands out of his face. But she wanted him to see her when she assured him that she held no judgment.

Lydia stepped up. The tips of her shoes nearly touched his boots. With two fingers, she gently pushed aside his hair as fine as capillaries.

Wesley's head shot up in surprise. His blue eyes that could be so piercing and yet so beautiful darkened into skepticism. He didn't trust her. Period. That sure didn't make her want to help him. In fact, she wouldn't be able to help him if he didn't tear down this wall of distrust. "I want nothing between us. If you want my help, then you need to be honest with me."

Wesley's shoulders relaxed a bit. "That's what I always told Jenny. I could only help her if she was honest with me."

"But she wasn't." Lydia hoped he would confide in her.

He hesitated, but he kept his stare steady on her. "I think she might've got me fired," he admitted quietly. "The night she came running to me for help was my last night on duty. At the time, I thought she loved me and could never hurt me. The idea that she set me up wouldn't even compute then. Now, I have to wonder."

"This was at the university?"

He studied her in silence. "I see you checked up on me."

Lydia shrugged. "Not really, but it does amaze me how some people talk so freely. I don't have that gift."

He smirked. "Maybe not that gift, but you have your own gifts. I'd say you're quite talented."

Lydia's heart expanded at his words, but she needed the rest of the story. Would he open up with her and share? "What happened that night?" she asked.

"I was working at the school's art museum as security. Some antique jewelry collection was stolen on my watch." His jaw ticked.

"Jewelry? As in rubies?"

Wesley shook his head. "I don't know. At the time, all I cared about was the fact that Jenny's father told the police it was me who stole them. I always figured it was him who set me up so I would disappear from his daughter's life. They didn't approve of her dating a pauper like me."

"I'm sorry."

He shrugged off her sympathy. "Doesn't

matter. The only thing that matters is figuring out what she was running from. Because if that skeleton is her, then whoever was following her might've caught up to her."

"But, Wesley, don't you see? If that skeleton is her..."

"I know. If that skeleton is her, then I'm first in line as a suspect."

Silence ensued. The crashing waves blurred into white noise as they stared at each other with the gravity of where this investigation was headed.

For Wesley, that might mean jail.

For Lydia, it could mean cracking a case that would put her name in headlines. Finally, on her own merits, and not on the coattails of her father. Elite family. Missing crown jewels. A little surge of excitement coursed through her at the possibility of where this could take her career. If nothing else, it could mean earning the promotion to directorship. The desire to say yes, for that reason alone, sat on her tongue.

Instead, she said, "If you're innocent, like you say you are, then this would be a huge cover-up involving a very prestigious and formidable Boston family."

"You know the Carmichaels?"

"I know of them. I grew up outside Boston and have seen their names in the papers enough times. This case *will* make headlines."

"It can't. Stepping Stones needs to be kept out of the media. This teaming-up together is covert. Got it?"

Her lips sealed tight as she remembered her promise to keep Stepping Stones out of the spotlight. That would mean no headlines. Maybe even no promotion.

"Watching you these past few days, Doc, I see you genuinely love your job. I love…" His face blanched. "I love the excitement I see in your eyes when you're working. It tells me you take your responsibility for finding the truth seriously. I see you're not out for fame."

Lydia's heart rate increased its pace. The sound pumped through her ears so loud she thought for sure Wesley would hear it. Her forced smile pulled on the flesh of her cheeks as her heart ached with the confliction of advancing her career over protecting these kind people. She thought of Len, who already escaped so much disruption in his life. Could she really bring more to their shores?

No, she couldn't. Not if she could help it. "Of course I'm not out for fame," she said. But did that include the promotion, she wondered.

"Good. Have Owen bring you to the station tomorrow morning at seven. We'll helicopter off the island first thing. Plan to spend a night or two."

"We can stay at my dad's house," she offered absently, her heart still fighting with her mind to let go of what she had hoped the Stepping Stones' case would be. Her own step up in her career. A step closer to obtaining her heart's desire.

"That works." Wesley continued with the plans, his voice melding with the white noise of the waves. "No hotel reservations to make our presence in town known. We can't forget there's a killer out there, and the more we close in on him or her, the more dangerous this becomes. The best thing for us all is to keep this off the record."

The best thing for them all? His words filtered into her thoughts. She wanted to make the best choices that would bring good, not harm, to Wesley's town. And even to Wesley. She was willing to put aside her career goals for it, but she had to wonder what Wesley would put aside. In particular, the wall of distrust around him. He still had yet to fully open up to her about his past. She let it go for now, but without his full honesty, she could very well be digging her own grave. And that didn't feel like it was the best thing for her.

FIVE

"You brought your tool kit?" Wesley came around his desk and relieved her of her overnight bag. He nodded to the case she held in front of her.

"I thought I might need it," Lydia said.

"I'm hoping not. You did bring the ruby, though, right? That we might need."

Lydia hesitated in her answer. The ruby was the only evidence that could lead to the killer. She wanted to trust that Wesley wasn't that person, but until all the facts were collected, she had to do the best job she could. And that included protecting the evidence.

But she also never lied.

"Got it," she said.

"Good. The helipad is out back." Wesley led the way through the station and out the back entrance. "Vaughn is prepping the chopper. He should be done by now."

She thought she heard him say, "Hopefully," but with the propellers of the helicopter rotating, she couldn't be sure she heard anything over the swirling blades cutting the early morning air.

"The door's open! Hop on and buckle up!" Wesley shouted to her. He met Deputy Vaughn halfway on the pad and shouted something to Derek, but Lydia missed it under the blade's whomping rotations. Whatever Wesley said, though, caused Derek to curl his lip at the sheriff's retreating back.

Her curiosity piqued, but when she climbed into the decrepit helicopter, her nosiness blew away with the stirred-up leaves and sand outside. She could have sworn she saw a similar green contraption on a rerun episode of *M.A.S.H.* She looked for the pilot up front, but both front seats were empty until Wesley came around the front and climbed into the pilot's seat.

"Wait!" She reached for the door handle, ready to bail. "Don't tell me you're flying this thing!" she shouted as loud as she could over the noise of the propellers.

Wesley picked up a set of large yellow headphones with a mouthpiece. He shook them at her, then pointed to a pair in the passenger seat up front. He wanted her to move up front?

She wanted off this whirling monster.

With his headphones on, Wesley flicked and checked switches. Obviously he'd done this before, but that didn't help her onslaught of hyperventilation.

Shaking legs carried her to the front seat; white knuckles grabbed on for dear life. Her mind raced with possible and horrible outcomes.

He tapped the headphones and mouthed, "Put them on," then tapped the watch at his wrist. Time was ticking—*away the minutes of her life!*

As soon as she fitted them to her head, she could hear his voice loud and clear. "You're looking a little pale, Doc. Ever fly a helicopter?"

She moved the mouthpiece and screeched, "Have *you?*"

His chuckle came through deep and smooth, melting her chilled nerves like ice cream trickled with warm fudge. "Many times. Sit back and enjoy the view. You're in for the ride of your life."

"That's what I'm afraid of. I like my quiet, *grounded* life."

"I imagine a life with skeletons is pretty quiet. And grounded." He chuckled again. "Get it? Grounded? Skeletons? In the ground."

She didn't laugh. "Not all of them. Some died in helicopter crashes over deep waters, nothing left but bones after the fish got to them."

He reached over and tapped her hand that clung to the seat's edge. His hand settled on hers, and he squeezed reassuringly. His touch was harmless enough and should have been comforting, but instead her breathing grew shallower.

"Hey, Lydia, you're okay. I won't let anything happen to you. Promise. Now breathe."

Lydia closed her eyes and followed his command. She let her tight lungs release their pent-up air, then refilled them with fresh new air. A few more cleansing breaths, and she let Wesley entwine his fingers into hers—but she still kept her eyes closed. "Okay, I can do this," she said into her microphone. "Even if I have to keep my eyes closed the whole time and go to my happy place."

He squeezed her hand one more time. When he withdrew, she knew it was time for lift-off. She nearly opened her eyes to tell him to let her out of this rickety thing, but his deep soothing voice came through the headphones and stopped her. "Tell me about your happy place. Where is it? What does it look like?"

"My lab." A surge of air entered her lungs at the mere mention of her workplace. She pulled the visual, speaking about a set of remains positioned on her white, lit table. "It's where I breathe the easiest."

Lydia felt her body lift off the ground in a smooth swoop. She was airborne and most likely already out over the water. Over deep wide-open dark water. She spoke louder to combat her fear. "Two hundred and six bones all laid out in their anatomically correct positions. Even the tiny stapes bone is there."

"Stapes bone? Where is that located?"

"It's the stirrup bone, one of the three auditory ossicles in the middle ear and the smallest human bone that enables a person to hear. Oh, speaking of which, when we get to Boston, I want to buy a book on sign language so I can sign with Miriam."

"I doubt you'll be on the island long enough to learn a language."

"You don't know me. When I set my mind to learn something, time means nothing."

"A real brain, are you?"

"Always have been."

They sat in silence for a while before Wesley's deep, soothing voice rumbled through her headphones again. "You're breathing better now. That must mean your stapes bone allowed you to hear me okay."

"Mmm…thank you for talking me down."

"Well, it's more like I talked you up."

"True, but don't remind me."

"I think you could probably open your eyes now. You're looking great—I mean not as pale," he corrected himself quickly. "I mean you look great, too, but that's not what I meant. I—"

She pried open one eye to witness the befuddled mess of his words. "Yes?"

"Nothing. Forget it."

The expanse of cerulean blue spread out before her and all else was forgotten. Both eyelids flashed open. On a gasp she leaned forward. Her stomach immediately flipped, and she flung herself back against the seat. "Wow." She observed the sea from her reserved position. "So unnerving…and yet… so beautiful."

"My sentiments exactly," he replied, but when she glanced in his direction, he wasn't looking at the water. He was looking at *her*. Or at least she thought he was. With his eyes disguised in his hair, she couldn't be sure.

Lydia plastered her head to the worn cushion. His statement confounded her. He had to be talking about the water. No one had ever put her in the same sentence as beautiful.

Smart, yes.

Tall, definitely.

Different, always.

But beautiful? Never.

Suddenly, this rattletrap wasn't her only unsafe dilemma. The direction of this conversation had taken on its own risky predicament. At this altitude and under her current vulnerability, a safer conversation was called for. "Do you and Deputy Vaughn not get along?" was the first idea that came to mind.

Wesley shrugged. "We get along fine. Why do you ask?"

"I noticed him give you an unpleasant look before we boarded. He didn't look happy with you."

"Oh, that's nothing. Just a difference in opinion."

"A difference in opinion could be huge to him. I have many differences of opinions with my boss. He probably shrugs them off just as easily as you do yours with Derek, but I know from my experience that Derek may not feel the same way."

"Isn't there only one way to assemble a skeleton? What kinds of differences do you have with your boss?"

Lydia chewed on her lower lip. How could

she explain when she didn't understand it herself? "He doesn't think I have what it takes. I graduated at the highest in my class. You would think that would give me bonus points, but nope, just ridicule. I think I only got the job because of who my father is. He's a pretty famous scientist, and I think Dr. Webber was expecting me to be as smart as my dad. I may not be, but that doesn't mean I'm not capable to do my job well." Lydia nearly mentioned the promotion, but thought better of the idea. Wesley was a smart man, and he would never trust her if he knew she wanted to advance her career. "In your case, I think Derek may take your differences in opinion a little more personal than you, so be aware. That's all."

"Except that's not all, Doc. I'll admit, I have my concerns with Vaughn, and they're justified. He can be too slow and not focused enough. That could put innocent people in harm's way. He's had a lot of mishaps that could have ended tragically for somebody. I keep him on desk duty and running errands because I don't have the manpower to fire him, but that doesn't mean I'm going to worry about how personal he takes my decisions. I have people's lives to consider. As the sheriff, I have decisions to make in the best interest of the job."

"I see." So much for safer conversation. Lydia cleared her throat and searched the horizon for another topic. "How much longer do you think?"

He cracked a smile. "Sorry. Didn't mean to make you more uncomfortable than you already are. It won't be long now. About fifteen minutes until landing."

"Really? Flying *is* much faster than taking the boat."

"That was the point. Glad you warmed to the idea. And see, everything worked out fine. We'll arrive with plenty of time to—" He leaned toward his gauges.

"Plenty of time for what?" she asked at his abrupt pause. She craned her neck to see what had his attention. She would need a manual and a little time to understand, but Wesley's pale complexion told her she didn't have either.

He tapped one of the gauges and mumbled, "That can't be."

"What can't be? Wesley, if this is a joke, I don't like it. I already hate flying in this archaic excuse for transportation as it is."

He didn't respond.

"Wesley, you're scaring me. What's going on?"

He frowned in thought as he flipped some switches. "It appears we're out of fuel."

Lydia flinched, her stomach clenched. "What does this mean?" She kept her eyes on Wesley instead of the deep dark waters below her. Panic swelled her throat, but she swallowed it down hard until the facts were presented. "Didn't you check it before we left?"

"Of course I checked it. We had a full tank. There should be a half tank left at this point. Plenty for the trip to Boston, and then some."

"So what are you saying?" She held out hope that things weren't as bleak as he made them sound.

"I'm saying if there was ever a time to panic it would be now."

That didn't sound very hopeful, she thought.

"I hope you like amusement park rides, Doc."

"No, I don't."

"That's too bad, because I have to perform an emergency auto rotation."

"What does that mean?"

"It means I have to take her down. Fast."

Wesley pushed the throttle forward at full force and plummeted the chopper in a downward sweep at about the same speed and aerodynamic stability as that of a fork-lift dropping from a bomber.

Lydia's stomach flew up to the sky as she raced to her death below. The deep, dark sea stood by, ready to swallow her alive.

Wesley jerked the throttle back just as they reached about twenty feet above the water's surface.

"You okay?" he asked a green-faced and silent Lydia as he reached for his radio to send out a mayday to the coast guard. The sputtering of the helicopter's propellers told him help wouldn't make it in time. He expected Lydia to cry and blame him for ruining her life. If there was a back door and a way out, he would expect her to take it and never look back. In this case, this lady would be justified in leaving him behind. But with no back door, she was stuck with him. And yet she didn't seem as angry about it as he expected.

She held her stomach and asked through cleansing breaths, "How long can we hover, you think?"

"I don't want to find out. If we go down with it, we'll sink real fast."

He yanked off his headset and unstrapped himself to reach behind his seat for a brand-new, never-used orange life jacket. He flung it at her and yelled over the motor barely chugging, "Put it on and let's go! The blades will turn on fumes for a few more rotations, but that's about it."

She removed her headset and followed his orders. "Where's yours?" she yelled back.

"No time!" Wesley leaned across her to unlatch her door. He pushed it wide. "Jump. Now!"

She turned around. "Wait! My tool kit! It's in the back!"

"Jump!" He pushed her closer to the door. He would push her all the way out if he had to, but her accepting nod told him it wouldn't be necessary.

Lydia moved to the door and ejected herself out without any countdown to prepare. He watched her splash, sink and bounce back up amid the spraying water below. He was surprised the blades still had enough power to swirl any water.

As soon as he let go of the throttle, the helicopter would spin out of control and crash into the sea. But if the blades stopped, the crash would come sooner. He had to get out before that happened.

Wesley glanced over his shoulder and saw Lydia's tool kit. Did he have time to make a grab for it? The ruby was in there. He had to try.

He leaned to his right as far as possible and with his left hand on the throttle, reached back with his right.

The tips of his fingers brushed the hard case. He felt the helicopter tip and brought his hand back in a flash to get it under control. He had to be crazy for even attempting such a fool thing.

Once more, he told himself, but that was it. He leaned back, reaching just a little bit farther. This time his fingers found the handle with success. Wesley pulled it up to the front just as the chopper's motor went completely silent. The fuel had run out, along with his time to escape.

The propellers sputtered one more rotation. Wesley shoved the door wide, but it flew back in his face when the helicopter rushed to the sea. He jammed the hard tool kit through the glass as the impact of metal meeting water jammed him to the ceiling. He ducked his head so his back took the brunt. The helicopter tipped on its side as it plunged down deep into darkening waters. He had to get out before it took him too far.

Water rushed in through the smashed window. He fought against a current so strong it would plunge him in seconds. With water reaching his nostrils, he tipped his head and inhaled the last of the remaining air and swam out and up with every ounce of strength.

The pinpoint of light pulled him forward. He kicked with his legs but swam with one hand. He hadn't realized he never let go of the tool kit. Should he now? It would give him a better chance of making it to the surface if he did.

But the ruby was in it. The only clue they had to identifying the skeleton. Plus, something in Wesley wanted to hand the case to Lydia. Not because of the stone, but because he knew it would make her happy. The vision of her face lighting up surged him forward—even when the last bit of air in his lungs dissipated.

The beckoning portal of light above didn't seem to get any closer. Wesley struggled to reach the opening as he struggled with the decision to let the case go. Maybe it would only be one more grasp.

Maybe it would be twenty.

Sparkles of light flickered in his vision. His aching lungs told him they were not from above but from within. The loss of oxygen would make up his mind for him.

"Wesley!" Icy salt water sloshed in Lydia's mouth as she screamed his name. In a frenzy she swam to the location where the hungry sea had swallowed the helicopter in one gulp.

"Please, God! Please help me. Help me find Wesley. Please save him." With each splash, thoughts of why he hadn't jumped circulated through her mind. What had he been waiting for?

Lydia swam hard and fast, stopping in what she hoped was the right place. The ocean felt infinite, so she couldn't be positive this was where he went down. She tried to swim under, but her life jacket buoyed her. A look into the water and a swivel around caught movement.

"Oh, please, God, let it be Wesley and not a shark."

She attempted another plunge, but the jacket reminded her of its existence. If she was going to help, it had to come off. Lydia unclicked the hinges to remove her arms from the holes, keeping one arm looped through to keep her afloat.

Another glance into the salty water burned her eyes. Her head popped out so her hands could rub the sting away. That's when she noticed her glasses were gone from her face.

A hindrance she'd deal with later. Once she and Wesley were rescued.

Lydia zeroed in on finding him. Another underwater search found him swimming up to her. Relief swept over her. He'd gotten out, after all. Any second, he would burst through.

But any second turned into too many seconds.

Something was wrong.

She sank her face back under the water and saw Wesley hadn't made any progress. Something held him back. Something in his hand that she couldn't make out in the murky water.

She would go to him, but to do so would mean letting go of what she held in her hand. Her only sure thing for staying afloat. She had to, though. She couldn't leave him down there and let him drown. The answer was simple.

She let go of the life jacket.

Lydia swam down. She could see Wesley's struggles slowed. *Don't give up!* She wished she could yell to him, but all she could do was swim down harder. She let some of her precious air out to allow herself to sink faster. Bubbles drifted up as she dropped farther down.

She reached his head, his hair strands waved and she could almost touch them. She noticed his arms stopped moving, or at least the arm closest to her. Another reach and she grabbed hold of it. Wesley's body jerked and tugged her down.

Her chest tightened in fear. She couldn't let him drown her!

Lydia yanked back with all her might, and more bubbles escaped her mouth. She kicked and pushed up, dragging him with her. He pushed back and she realized he was kicking his way up, too.

It wasn't much farther now. The shimmering glass surface was within reach. *Hang on, Wesley! God, give him Your strength!* She glanced down and saw how wide his eyes were. He had nothing left. She kicked harder and turned her gaze back to where air awaited them. Except now the shimmering glass surface had turned white and foamy.

Lydia broke through to have water spraying

her in the face. She inhaled little intakes of air when what she really needed was whole lungfuls. It took her a second, and a loud motor above, to figure out what was happening around her.

The coast guard had arrived. *Thank You, Lord!*

Wesley burst through beside her, his loud inhale sounded painful. His hand grabbed at her shoulders.

"Wesley, it's okay! Help is here. Please don't push me down," she shouted through the pelting of the water from the hovering helicopter. Water sloshed in her mouth from his dunks. She paddled her hands and kicked her feet without ceasing to stay afloat, especially when his erratic breathing and bug-eyed stare scared her into thinking he might not understand and accidently hurt her.

A ladder fell beside them. Lydia looked up to see a rescuer climbing out of the helicopter above to come down to their aid.

"Help's on the way. Hang on to the ladder. It will help you," she instructed him, and he thankfully let go of her shoulder for the ladder. Wesley's other arm lifted from the water, and Lydia saw what kept him weighted down.

Her forensic tool kit.

"Wesley! Why do you have this?" she shouted over the chopper's noise. "You could have drowned!"

His breathing steadied a bit for him to answer, "I thought...I thought you would be happy... It has the ruby in it."

Lydia shook her head and grabbed at the collar of her soaked sweater. She reached in and pulled out a string around her neck.

The ruby hung from it between them.

"But you said—" Wesley stilled, even his short breaths subsided. His eyebrows knitted together, and then his jaw tightened. "Oh, I get it. You lied!"

The rescuer reached them and extended an arm. "Ladies first!"

Lydia shook her head emphatically, the word *no* on her lips, but her answer was meant for Wesley, not the rescuer. Even so, the rescuer hoisted her up under her arms. "Wesley!" she hollered down to him as she grabbed hold of the rope ladder.

"We have to move, ma'am!" the rescuer shouted in her ear, jolting her to move up the ladder. Her hands shook with each hold and release. Her vision blurred, but from more than the absence of her glasses. Unshed tears welled up. She squeezed her eyes tight to diminish them. At the top rung, she searched below for the man who didn't believe in her. Her pleas wouldn't matter. Her actions wouldn't hold water. In his mind, she was untrustworthy. She was as credible with Wesley as she was with Dr. Webber. Neither man thought she was capable of much, so why did she bother to try so hard? Why bother at all?

SIX

"Thank you for buying me some clothes." Lydia stepped out of the ladies' room at the security office of Boston's airport and took the vinyl seat beside Wesley in the waiting area. Since her overnight bag was swimming with the fishes, along with her wallet, Wesley bought her a gray sweatshirt and pants with Property of Boston Red Sox stamped on the front and down the leg.

"Sorry, they're men's," he said. "The stores in the airport didn't offer sizes for tall women."

"That's okay. We match." Lydia smiled, referring to the same ensemble Wesley wore. When he didn't return her smile, she let hers slide. "Anyway, when we get to my dad's house, I'll pay you back."

"Don't worry about it. I can swing it. Besides, it's the least I can do after nearly killing you."

"I have a feeling it wasn't you that nearly killed me, or I should say *us*."

"I'd have to concur with your assessment, Doc. I've been sitting here trying to figure it out. I've made that flight a thousand times. I've never run out of fuel. That fuel line was most assuredly cut."

"You must really have made Deputy Vaughn mad about something."

"Why do you think it was Vaughn who cut the line?"

"He was the one to prep the helicopter. If he didn't cut the line, wouldn't he have at least noticed?"

He raised his eyebrows without a reply.

"Oh, right. Lack of focus. In his defense, though, you did kind of rush him this morning."

Wesley's jaw ticked. "Perhaps, Doc, you're not in the position of playing judge. You'd have to be honest for such an honorable title."

"I am honest, and we've already gone through this—"

"Right. You were wearing the ruby so you could keep it safe. Apparently, that means safe from me. But speaking of which, are you still wearing it? And I'm not asking because I plan to swipe it."

Her hand went to her throat where the makeshift necklace and ruby were covered by her sweatshirt. "Of course, why?"

"I'd like to make a stop after this at Jenny's house. Talk to her parents. Maybe show them the jewel to see if they remember anything about it."

"Like *this?*" Lydia waved her hand at her attire. She scrunched her face at the idea of knocking on someone's door to talk about their dead daughter in a sweat suit.

"What? It was better than the pink set. At least you don't look like a tall strawberry milkshake."

"Right, because the gray elephant at their door will be much more reputable."

Wesley scoffed. "Doc, you don't have to ever worry about someone mistaking you for an elephant. A giraffe, maybe."

Lydia sent him a scathing look.

"Oops, sorry, forgot. Sore subject."

She let his reference go on a long exhale. "Let's just go. Do you want me to call for a car?"

"I can hail a taxi."

"A taxi? We cannot show up in sweatpants and a taxi and expect admittance into one of these homes. We should at least arrive in a Town Car."

"For someone who doesn't have a wallet, you sure are a big spender. I'm not authorized to spend that kind of money. As it is, I just cost the island an expensive aircraft."

"Expensive? That rattletrap should have been retired with the Vietnam War."

"Well, excuse me. I didn't realize our means of transport needed to be fit for royalty."

"Not royalty, just precious life!"

Wesley turned his face away to the blurred sign on the wall. She thought it said something about airport rules, but without her glasses she couldn't be sure. The only thing she could read were the remorseful signs Wesley exhibited with his blotching cheeks.

"Sorry," she said. "You don't need me making you feel guiltier over something that wasn't your fault to begin with."

With him still giving her his side view, she watched his Adam's apple bob with a deep, silent swallow.

She stood. "I'll be right back. I'm going to call for a car, and it won't cost you anything. Consider it on me." Lydia walked to the front desk and asked to use the phone. She would have to get her cell phone replaced right after the visit to the Carmichaels'. She couldn't be out of touch from her office. Within twenty minutes, a black Town Car pulled up at the entrance to pick them up. Wesley gave the chauffeur a snide look as the man held the door.

"Hello, Lydia," the chauffeur said, a slight smile to his look of professionalism. His gaze only settled on her attire for a split second. "It's wonderful to see you. You have me at your service all day. Where would you like to go?"

"Beacon Street," Wesley answered for her.

"It's nice to see you, too, Charlie." Lydia

smiled at the chauffeur as she entered the backseat.

Wesley followed her in. "You two know each other?" He eyed Charlie as he made his way around the car and climbed in.

"Yes, we go way back."

"He's kind of old for you, don't you think?"

"It's not like that."

"Then how is it?"

Lydia opened her mouth to explain Charlie was like a member of the family, but when she noticed Wesley scrutinizing the back of Charlie's head, she snapped shut. If he didn't trust her anyway, then she didn't have much to live up to. "I don't believe it's any of your business."

"Well, that's the first time you've told the truth today, Doc."

She flinched. She didn't like the way his distrust in her made her feel so inconsequential. It made her question if she was able to help him at all. If she even wanted to.

Jeeves, or Charlie, or whoever was carting them around in this snooty stretch, pulled the car to a stop at the curb and parked it. Brownstone manors lined the street on both sides. Mature trees with their wide trunks and elongated branches reached across the street and stood out front as proud and elegant as the stately homes they guarded. Tall front steps made of marble extended down from elaborate entranceways. Black ironwork balustrades swept up the sides of the steps, seeming to welcome passersby to take hold and come inside, but Wesley doubted many people actually ever gained access.

He knew he never did.

The chauffeur exited to come around and open the door for them, but Wesley reached for the handle. "I can open my own door," he told Lydia sitting beside him.

"Just let him do his job. It's not going to hurt you."

"I don't depend on anyone for anything." He pulled the door latch before Charlie reached him.

"Wait." Lydia grabbed his forearm. "Someone's coming out of the Carmichaels' home."

Wesley stayed put behind tinted windows

and sized up a man with a black baseball cap. Light brown hair, about five-eleven and wearing a black leather coat, the collar of his coat pulled high to shield half his face. The other half was shielded with big black sunglasses. He crossed the street right in front of their Town Car and got into the driver's seat of another black fancy-shmancy car.

"Good idea about renting the Town Car to come to this neighborhood," Wesley conceded. "The guy didn't look twice at us. We fit right in."

In any second, he expected Lydia to take her glory and say, I told you so, but, instead she was too busy staring at the guy's car as he sped down the street behind them. When he turned at the end of the street, she faced forward slowly, her teeth biting her lower lip. Charlie opened the door, but Miss Oblivious didn't notice.

"Is there a problem, Doc?"

She jerked. "No. I don't know. Maybe." She looked at him, or more like through him. She seemed to be focusing on an image from another time and place.

"Another man from your past?"

Lydia shook her head. "Do you know him?"

"Me? How would I know him?"

"Well, it's hard to tell because my vision is slightly blurred, but I think I saw him on Stepping Stones."

"I highly doubt it. I would know if he's been on my island."

"You're probably right." But she didn't seem put at ease, especially when she stole another look over her shoulder before following him out the door, and then every few steps up to the front door.

"That guy really got to you. What aren't you telling me?" Wesley asked before he rang the doorbell.

"I'm sure it's nothing. I..." She sighed. "You're going to think I'm crazy."

"It wouldn't take much."

"I'm being serious."

Wesley gave a sharp nod. "All right, then. I'm listening."

"I think that was the man who tried to steal my tool kit the morning after I arrived on the island. I can't be sure because I didn't get a good look, but I remember the hat and sunglasses."

Wesley hit the doorbell.

"You don't believe me." Lydia sighed. "I'm telling you the truth."

"Well, now you're going to think *I'm* crazy, because I actually do believe you." He had to. What kind of cop would he be if he ignored the distress in her eyes? What kind of man would he be? "Could be a coincidence, but if it's not and that *is* the guy who tried to steal your kit, the fact that he just exited the Carmichaels' home, marks this spot with a giant X." He jabbed his thumb in the direction of the muffled footsteps they could hear approaching behind the closed door. "Get your shovel ready, Doc. Our digging starts now."

"May I help you?" The butler's scrutinizing eyes latched on to their matching sweat suits, then pinched his lips in disdain.

Lydia watched Wesley flash his badge in his wallet for a split second. The leather exhibited dried patches, but for the most part, it still was bloated with water. "Yes," he said.

"I'm with the police department and I need to speak with Mr. Carmichael."

"I'm sorry. Mr. Carmichael is not here. Do you have an appointment? Perhaps you would like to leave your card. I will be sure he receives it."

"I'm sure you would, but if Mr. Carmichael isn't here, I'll talk to the missus instead?"

"What is this in reference to?" The butler closed the door a few inches.

"It's a private matter." Wesley put his foot on the threshold.

"Something tells me you're not with the police. What did you say your name was?"

"Sheriff Grant...and I didn't."

"Sheriff Grant." The man said Wesley's name as though it tasted like sewage. "You will have to call to make an appointment. Good day."

"Wait, sir." Lydia jumped to intercede for Wesley's fine botching skills. She should have known the bulldog would have as much finesse as his species warranted. "I'm Dr. Lydia Muir, a forensic anthropologist with the medical examiner's office in Maine. I'm conducting an investigation on a skeleton that has been found. It's very important that we speak to one of the Carmichaels today."

"I cannot fathom what the Carmichaels have to do with your investigation. You most assuredly have the wrong people."

"Perhaps, but just in case, I need to question them about what they know about this." Lydia revealed the stringed ruby from behind her sweatshirt. The color of bloodred dripped from her fingertips and reflected Boston's sunshine off its glassy surface.

The butler swallowed so hard she heard the gulp. He widened the door. "Come in."

Lydia stepped past Wesley. She took the opportunity to flash him a smug smile.

Except it went wasted.

Wesley only had eyes for the stone at her neck. Hateful eyes. Was his aversion directed at the gem? Or was it for the woman who once wore it?

Quickly, Lydia sheathed it back behind its cotton shield, unsure of what it might make him capable of. She still couldn't rule the good sheriff out as a suspect. Making this trip with him was turning out to be a bad idea all around.

They stopped in the center of a huge tiled foyer. A wide staircase swept up in a curve before them, its banister shining like glass. She took a step closer and her shoe tripped on a divot in the floor. Upon closer inspection, she noticed three more, each three feet apart.

A table used to stand here. Probably a round table, laden with a vase and fresh-cut flowers. The question she had was, where did it go? Out to be repaired?

"Please, wait here," the butler instructed, and ascended the stairs with the fast taps of his polished shoes. He reached the top floor and passed by a tall wall where a swash of blue in the shape of a rectangle was a few shades darker than the rest of the pale walls. It looked as though a picture had hung from there recently. Had it also been sent out for repair or cleaning?

Or were the Carmichaels selling off their possessions?

"Fool," Wesley whispered harshly at her from behind.

Lydia jerked at the verbal assault. The guy didn't let up. She whipped her head to confront him, expecting to meet him nose to nose. Instead she met his lifted chin. He was looking at the ceiling. "Did you just call me a fool?"

He dropped his head to meet her eyes. "No. I called myself a fool. I can't believe I ever thought I stood a chance with her."

"Who?"

"Jenny. *This* is what she was used to." He flung an arm to insinuate the elaborate surroundings, even with the missing pieces. "Look at that chandelier. Are those diamonds?"

She looked up. "No, I'm sure they're crystal."

"Whatever. It's no wonder she left me. I'd leave me, too, if all I had to offer was a rundown two-bedroom cabin on a stinky fishing island."

"I don't think Stepping Stones smells."

He twisted his lips with imminent sarcasm. "This coming from the one who hangs out in a morgue surrounded by roadkill fumes. No offense, but your nose isn't exactly trustworthy."

She crossed her arms at her chest. "So now my nose has to earn your trust, too? You're unbelievable."

"I would have to agree," a woman's voice interrupted from the top of the staircase. Lydia turned her attention to an elegant woman practically floating down the stairs in a pressed white suit. "The fact that you would show your face in my home is quite unbelievable." The woman took the last step right up to Wesley.

"Mrs. Carmichael." He nodded but didn't smile. "I can assure you, I'm only here because the circumstances warranted such a visit."

"And what circumstances would those be?" Her lips pinched so tight they nearly matched her suit.

"We are here to exhume Jennifer's casket."

Mrs. Carmichael sputtered. Tinged hysteria flashed in her gray eyes. "Exhume? What are you talking about? There is no casket to exhume."

"I'm sorry?" Wesley sent a quick confused look in Lydia's direction. "I was told she was buried here in Boston."

"Well, you were told wrong. My daughter's body was never recovered from the sea."

Air rushed out of Wesley. Lydia recognized a moment of paralysis in his ability to respond and stepped in to help. "Mrs. Carmichael, I'm Dr. Lydia Muir—"

"Muir…Do I know that name?" The woman sized her up with squinty gray eyes.

"I don't know, but what I do know is skeletal remains of a young woman have been unearthed on Stepping Stones Island, as well as an item we believe belonged to your daughter."

"My butler mentioned something about a ruby. Let's see it."

Lydia reached into the collar of her sweatshirt and withdrew the gem again. She let it lie flat against the fabric. The woman's eyes bulged for a few beats.

"Do you recognize it?" Lydia asked.

Mrs. Carmichael mumbled something about calling her husband. Then out loud said, "I'm not positive. My husband would be able to find out. He has a business associate who deals with the gem collections at the museum, which is where Calvin, my husband, is now. He's getting ready for the gala tonight. Perhaps I can hold on to the stone for the day until he's had a chance to look at it. I know he is familiar with rubies especially."

Mrs. Carmichael stepped close, infringing on Lydia's personal space while her gaze devoured the gem. Lydia quickly slipped it back out of view. What was up with this stone and its effects on people? The menacing reactions caused the ruby to practically burn against her flesh.

"No, I'm sorry," she said, "but this stone is evidence and could identify the skeleton it was found with. I can't let it out of my sight."

Wesley stepped close to her arm, brushing against her reassuringly. "Can you tell us who this business associate is?" he asked Mrs. Carmichael.

The woman looked affronted. "Why would I be involved with my husband's affairs?"

"Because you're married," Lydia said. "You must help him in some ways, don't you?"

"That's what he has his consultants for. I am much too busy in my own endeavors, especially with my hours of volunteering with the many humanitarian foundations I'm a part of. I work very hard to fund-raise for awareness on issues of human atrocities. And speaking of which, tonight's art gala is one of these fund-raisers that I must get ready for. I really must ask you to be on your way."

"But, Mrs. Carmichael, we still have some questions—"

"I can't help you." Mrs. Carmichael's words raced from tight lipstick-lined lips. "You need to leave now. Walter! Please escort these people out."

The butler reappeared from behind the stairs, coming to his mistress's rescue. At the moment he seemed more like her bodyguard with his hands ready to reach out and grab them.

Wesley's hands went up, palms open. "Whoa, hold on there, Walt. We're on our way out. No need to get pushy. Let's go, Lydia. I think we got everything we came for."

"No, we didn't."

"Now, Lydia." His voice held no leeway for negotiation. His hand encircled her upper arm and tugged her back to the door.

"But we need to speak with Mr. Carmichael. I have a few more questions. I—"

She saw the gun.

Her focus had been on Mrs. Carmichael, so she'd missed the butler exposing his sidearm from under his suit coat. He didn't draw it, but did she really want to wait to find out if he would?

Lydia's mouth went dry, and she was stunned speechless. She stumbled as Wesley dragged her out through the door and down the stairs.

"Open the door, Charlie," Wesley called out to the chauffeur, who waited by the car. "Then get in the driver's seat. This is no time for extravagant service. We'll shut the door ourselves."

Lydia's shocked reaction wore off enough for her to pick her feet up and move swiftly toward the car. Even so, Wesley still held on to her. In fact, he'd pushed her in front of him and out of the line of view from the door. He used his body as a shield, and she didn't think it was done by accident.

At the rear door, she climbed and slid over to the other side of the seat so Wesley could get in. The car took off like a bullet, smooth and sleek, down the tree-lined road that suddenly felt like a facade.

"Trouble back there?" Charlie checked his rearview mirror.

"Could have been worse," Wesley answered.

"Where to now?" Charlie inquired.

Wesley stared out the window at the city of Boston passing by. "Do you mind dropping us off at Boston Common? I think we need to get out and walk for a while."

"It's a nice day for a walk, I'd say." Charlie hit the blinker switch. "But I won't just drop you off. I'll hang around and wait. Like I said, I'm at your service all day."

"That's really not necessary, Charlie. Honestly, I can't pay for such a service."

"Pay?"

"I told you I had it covered," Lydia broke in, welcoming the new train of thought. Anything to get her mind off that gun…and the danger she could be in sticking with Wesley and his covert investigation.

He angled an annoyed look at her. "You have no money. Remember?"

Lydia sighed and dropped her head back on the seat. "Charlie works for my father. Okay? It's not costing me anything. My dad is taking care of it."

He squinted at her through his disheveled hair. "Why the big secret? Why not just say so?"

"I believe you agreed it was none of your business."

"That's not what I meant and you know it."

"Fine. You're right. You win! I give up. Okay? Happy now?" Lydia raised her hand to insinuate she wasn't in the mood to spar with him. It trembled between them, shaking like a lone leaf on an extended branch. A sign her nerves were stretched beyond control.

In silence, Wesley took her hand in his own. Linked, he brought them down on the cool leather seat between them. "I'm sorry," he whispered, tightening his hold on her and soothing her nerves. "I take it you've never been threatened with a gun."

Lydia shook her head once. "You would think because I deal with guns daily, I would have reacted with more bravado."

"You don't deal with guns. You deal with the aftermath. You know enough to be fearful of people who misuse them."

Lydia inhaled deeply and mumbled, "No promotion is worth dying over."

"Promotion? What promotion?"

She looked out the window, remembering she gave that dream up to protect the people of Stepping Stones from an entourage of media. "I meant my job," she corrected. "My job isn't worth dying over. In fact, it's not supposed to be dangerous at all."

"I'm sorry I got you into this. I promised you on the helicopter I wouldn't let anything happen to you, and now I've messed up twice, badly. I would understand if you want to call it quits and head back to your lab. I won't keep you here."

Going back would guarantee failure. It would be proof that she wasn't capable, after all. It would also mean handing over this case to someone else who *would* put Stepping Stones in the headlines.

She'd promised Wesley she would keep the island protected, but this was bigger than she'd thought. If this skeleton was a Carmichael, there was no way Stepping Stones would escape the press. But she might be able to keep it low-key.

Charlie pulled up to the Common. The early spring lawns rolled and stretched far and wide. A collection of artists, pedestrians and tourists filled the pathways. The swan boats carried people across the shimmering lagoon and around the newly flowering gardens, bursting with new life and beauty. God's handiwork. The scene brought her some peace from the life-threatening situations she found herself in today.

"Thank you for bringing me here," she whispered aloud. "It's peaceful and reminds me God is with me. I have nothing to fear. He's led me here and wouldn't have brought me here if He didn't have a reason. He's put this ball in motion, and it'll take a greater force than me to stop it now. If He's okay with me being here, then I'm okay." She sighed with her answer. "I'm not going back to my lab. I'm going to see this case through. But—" She squeezed Wesley's hand to halt him from responding. She wasn't done yet. "But, Wesley, it's not a coincidence that you're on this path, too. He *is* leading you."

"You sound like my mother with all her Proverbs. They didn't help her, and they're not going to help me." Wesley let go of her hand to reach inside his pocket. He withdrew his wallet, pulling out various wet bills. "But I am glad you're staying. Here."

"You're paying me for sticking with you?" She eyed the green he pushed into her hand.

"No. You need to buy a dress. Have you ever crashed a party?"

"Me? I would never think of doing such a thing."

"Because you think it would be wrong or because the idea of going to a party gives you the hives?"

Lydia had to think about that one, but in the end, the answer came easy. "The hives."

"That's what I thought. Be back here by six. Bring some anti-itch cream if you have to." He grabbed the handle.

"Wait, you can't just crash an art gala. You need tickets. Do you want to end up in jail?"

"It wouldn't be the first time Carmichael's tried to put me there."

"Then all the more reason to get tickets." Lydia called to the front, "Charlie, can you get us two tickets to the Carmichael art gala?"

Charlie lifted his cell phone to dial. "Sure can."

She looked back at Wesley, who didn't look pleased. "Those tickets have to be a couple thousand dollars each. I can't—"

"I didn't ask you to. Let me help you, but, Wesley, you *have* to trust me. Can you do that?"

He stood in the doorway with no answer for her. It wasn't a no, but it wasn't a yes, either. He pushed his hair back, and the sunshine glittered in his blue eyes. So much conflict reflected back, but then he dropped his hair just as she thought she recognized something else. Pain?

"Be back here at six. Come dressed to impress." With that he scattered faster than the pigeons did when he slammed the door behind him.

SEVEN

"That is the dress." Stacia, the boutique owner, ran over to Lydia and swept down the long, draping chiffon skirt. "Red is your color, and with your height you bring a regal quality to a dress that has hung lifeless on my racks for months. It's like it was waiting for you. Just lovely."

Lydia studied herself in the trifold mirror. A numerous red-gown kaleidoscope reflected at her as each mirror multiplied her image. She pointed the matching red shoes out in front of her, then tucked them back under the floor-length skirt. "I've never worn a red dress before. I tend to pick colors like blue and black and brown. Are you sure about this?"

"Oh, I'm positive. With your rich chest-nut-colored hair and that glorious ruby at your neck, the color pops. Everyone will notice you."

"That's what I'm afraid of." Lydia chewed on her lower lip.

Stacia paused in her fuss. She looked up at Lydia and placed her small dainty seamstress hand on Lydia's cheek. "Your humbleness is a virtue I don't see much of anymore. These girls these days come in here and want gowns that will not only get them noticed, but offer shock value. But you…You stand here so noble and modest. And so very beautiful. You have brought me such joy today. Thank you for coming into my store."

Lydia smiled down at the woman. "Thank you for saying such nice things." Another glimpse at the stranger in the mirror and Lydia raised her chin and nodded once in determination. "Okay. I can do this."

"I know you can, but first, I think I might have a chain that will fit that ruby. The string kind of ruins the dress. And we can't have that." Stacia swept from her side for the jewelry counter, returning with a short gold roped chain and scissors.

"It's beautiful, Stacia, but I only have a certain amount of money on me."

"Don't worry. I'll give you a good discount." She snipped the string before Lydia could object. Lydia caught the ruby before it fell, and within seconds, it looked right at home attached to the gold chain. "This is a good, strong clasp. You won't lose your gem with this chain. I guarantee it." Stacia secured it at the back of Lydia's neck and the ruby fell right at Lydia's clavicle bone. "Perfect. Well, almost perfect."

Lydia groaned. "What now?"

"The hair. Why so tight? Let me loosen it for you." Stacia pulled a chair to the mirror and Lydia sat so the short woman could take out the pins that kept her sensible bun together. Her hair swept down her back, and with deft hands, Stacia had it twisted and pinned back up just as the clock struck six.

"I'm late!" Lydia jumped from the chair. She scooped up the sweat suit and dug into the pocket for Wesley's money. She was sure when Wesley saw her he would think she had chosen well and had been a good steward with what he had. She knew this was his own money and not the town's. A kind sentiment, but she still planned to pay him back every penny. "Is this enough?" She handed it to Stacia, who counted it and smiled.

"It's fine. Now let me walk you to the door. You seem a little wobbly in those heels, and those are the shortest ones I have."

Stacia gave the glass door a push, jingling the bell overhead. She reached to give Lydia a quick hug, then pulled back to squeeze her hands. "Your man will be quite pleased."

"Oh, he's not my man," Lydia objected as she stepped out onto the sidewalk.

Stacia chuckled. "Well, maybe he's not your man yet, but once he sees you in that dress, that will all change."

Lydia felt the heat of a blush travel up her neck as she waved off Stacia's silly comment and headed back to the Common. As if a pretty dress could catch Wesley's eye. The idea was preposterous. Ludicrous.

So then why was she still thinking about it?

She turned the corner and hit the walk signal button, her thoughts such a jumble of confusion that she barely noticed the people around her. At the signal, she crossed the street and noticed some people staring at her from the other side. She looked over her shoulder to see if they stared at something behind her, but the people behind her were looking at her, too.

Huh, maybe Stacia was right and the dress *would* catch Wesley's eye. Lydia smiled to herself and picked up her step to the curb, but when her feet wobbled, she remembered slow and steady wins the race.

Not that there was a race to win a prize or Wesley. Although he was a handsome man, and she did have this grade-school attraction to him, a relationship with him would be tedious. She knew if she wore braids he would be pulling them all the time. A constant battle, for sure. No way would she put herself through that. He would have to… Lydia stopped her ridiculous train of thought and took a turn onto a cut-through path to get to the other side of the Common where her nondate waited. Never had Wesley even hinted at a possibility of there being something more between them. Why was her mind flittering to such a place?

It had to be what Stacia had said. The sweet old woman's words tricked Lydia into believing she might be the wallflower that gets picked at the ball this time. *Silly Stacia, tough guys like Wesley don't date science geeks.*

Lydia's shoe caught on a sidewalk crack, tripping her out of her youthful fancies and sending her forward for a face-plant. In quick response, she bent her knees and stabilized her tall body to stop the fall. She looked behind her to see if anyone noticed.

Phew, no one noticed because no one was around. She'd left the crowds back on the main walk for this secluded shortcut. She needed to hurry, but she also needed to watch her step, especially with her blurred vision.

Lydia faced back around and caught the sight of a man all in black. He stood up ahead on the path. She hadn't noticed him before and wouldn't have cared except he blocked her way, not moving.

She squinted, but the distance was too far and the early evening sun flashed out any of his identifying features. His arms hung down by his sides but slowly began to move to his chest. He folded them there. A threatening stance that kept her feet locked in place.

Lydia peered to her left for another way across the Common. A cut through the public gardens might be a better choice than passing by this man—if he let her pass, that is.

But then how far would she get in dirt mounds with heels? If he came after her, then it wouldn't be very far at all.

Lydia opened her mouth to ask what he wanted, but her voice lost its power. Her lips moved with nothing but scared silence between them. Her only chance was to run back to the street and crowds.

Slowly, she knocked off her shoes under her dress. They would be left behind when she made her mad dash. Her fingers gripped the fabric of her dress, but before she could lift the hem to make a run for it, the man spoke.

"I see you're still falling flat on your face, Doc."

Wesley.

Air expelled from Lydia's lungs in a rush.

She let go of the skirt, but her fists stayed bunched. She put her shoes back on under the skirt and marched the rest of the way up to him as she spoke her mind. "I don't appreciate you scaring me like that."

"I wasn't scaring—" He stopped when she reached him and they came face-to-face. His eyes turned from their typical pugnaciousness to inquisitive. He searched her face as she searched his.

Something was wrong with this picture, though. Then it hit her.

She could see his eyes.

"You cut your hair!" She reached up to touch the blond strands neatly hanging to his sides from a center part. Just as her fingertips made contact, he grabbed her wrist and held it there between them.

Lydia swallowed hard at the intensity of his gaze. Had she overstepped a boundary? "I'm sorry," she started. "I…I wasn't going to mess it up. I'm just so excited to see your whole face." She let a genuine smile come, unable to hold it back if she tried. She was staring at one beautiful man. "You look great. Nice tux."

He dropped her hand and stepped back. "You're late. I didn't think you were coming back. I thought maybe you decided to bail, after all."

"Hey, it takes a while for a girl to get ready and look like a million bucks." She smiled and mock-curtsied to show off her dress.

He barely dropped his gaze. She didn't think he even looked at her dress. Then in a quick pivot, he gave her his back and walked away.

Lydia's mouth fell open while she froze in place from his insult. His broad shoulders draped in crisp black pulled tighter with each rapid step of his black shiny shoes. Had touching his hair really made him that angry? So angry he couldn't return the compliment she'd given him? Not even a "You clean up well, Doc" or "Nice dress"?

Her hands swept down the chiffon gown as she remembered sweet Stacia's words. *"He may not be your man now, but once he sees you in that dress that will all change."*

"Looks like you were wrong, Stacia. Looks like I've been passed over again," Lydia mumbled as she made her way to the car. But this time, it was fine with her. She'd rather stay an unpicked wallflower than to be chosen by someone who only wanted to cut her down.

Wesley trudged up the art museum's stone staircase and wished for his hair back. His footing slowed its pace because of what awaited him behind the heavy doors.

His past.

He stopped, then faced the woman his mind was tricking him into thinking might be his future.

When he'd sat in the barber chair, his thoughts had been on one thing only. Making this amazingly beautiful woman beside him smile. And for a moment it worked. She beamed brighter than the sun. So stunning. So vibrant.

Then he saw what hung from her neck.

Jenny's ruby.

When he saw it on her at the Common, old anger from when Jenny had kept it between them reared up. But now, here at the museum, he couldn't turn away from the horrid thing as he had done at the Common. He would have to do his best to ignore it. He and Lydia had to track Calvin Carmichael down tonight. At the art gala, Carmichael wouldn't be able to deter them.

Wesley raised his gaze from the ruby to Lydia's face. His heart calmed only to speed up for a different reason. The woman was lovely. Gorgeous. The idea of having her on his arm tonight, even as a front, filled him with pride. In her elegance, he'd much rather show her off someplace else other than this despicable place. He would take her to the theater, then to a tucked-away treasure in Boston's North End where they could eat by candlelight and he could get lost in the way the flame reflected off her eyes.

Except it would also reflect off the loathsome jewel at her throat.

It amazed him that the bloodred stone still taunted him and had him seeing a red rage after all these years. It also reminded him of why he was back in Boston at all.

"We should talk about what to expect tonight," he said, focusing his mind back to business.

She straightened to her full height, her thin, milky shoulders shifted into a perfect and flattering posture. She looked at him with hesitance. He knew his actions at the Common hadn't been fair to her, but right now he needed to prepare her for what might go down at this shindig.

He tossed his head in the direction of the doors. "The people that attend these galas don't care for outsiders and tend to be pushy and rude."

"You should fit right in, then." Her eyes flashed fire as flaming as the ruby.

Wesley stood motionless for a few beats, then slowly cracked a smile. He tried not to, but he loved her quick wit. She didn't put up with his bad attitude at all.

But for how long?

At what point would his bad attitude poison her? Change her? Another reason to keep her at bay.

But for tonight, he had to keep her safe.

"Here's your warning, Doc. Don't stray far. There are a lot of dark corners in this archaic place. Bad things tend to happen in dark corners."

"You know this from experience. Will you tell me about it?"

Was this a game of Truth or Dare? It felt like both. He reached for his hair, but it was gone. There wouldn't be any more hiding.

On a sigh, he forced out, "This is where I used to work and where I was framed for stealing the aristocrat's collection. I went back to Stepping Stones with my tail between my legs."

"Why didn't you prove your innocence? That doesn't sound like you. You would have trounced to ensure justice."

Wesley gave a short laugh. "You seem to have me all figured out."

"Am I wrong?"

"You're right. I wanted to. I wanted my name cleared from any wrongdoing. They couldn't prove I did it, so no charges were brought, but with these people, they don't need charges to condemn. I was fired and my name was smeared for at least a hundred miles if not more. I couldn't get another job. I was done. So I had to go back to Stepping Stones."

"Why didn't you want to go back to Stepping Stones? I'm sure the islanders were ecstatic to have you back."

"Yeah, they were. Voted me in as sheriff immediately."

"Then why didn't you want to go back?"

He closed his eyes for a moment, then reopened them to Lydia's expectant eyes. He sighed and admitted his failure. "I hadn't been back since my mom's funeral. I guess you could say I hadn't actually lived up to my parents' expectations of me. My dad was a great sheriff. My mom was loved by all."

"I see."

"Do you?"

"More than you know." Lydia dropped her gaze to her pressed-together hands. "I struggle with living in the shadow of my father, too. He's a great scientist. I hope I can be just like him when I grow up." She lifted her face with understanding in her eyes and not a bit of condemnation. Then her beautiful lips curled at the edges.

Wesley relaxed at the sight. So welcoming they were. If he stayed out here on the steps a moment longer, he wouldn't be able to stop from kissing them.

Grant, you've got it bad. Stay focused. She is not your future. She's your charge. That is all.

Wesley turned to continue the rest of the way up the steps to the front doors. Dusk cast a shadow over the stairs. Darkness loomed, and so did an unnerving feeling of something else. More danger.

He opened the door and waved a hand for her to enter before him. "Remember what I said. Stick to the light."

"Always," she answered without pause. "But I know you don't mean the light of God, even if He *is* our guiding light."

"Yours," Wesley replied, and held out his arm as he'd wanted to do the moment he saw her approach him in the Common.

"Then it's a good thing I'm helping you. Because if God is lighting my path, then that means I'm bringing the lamp." She looped her arm elegantly through his and smiled brightly into his eyes. She fit perfectly beside him.

His stomach flipped at the idea, and he had to look away. He led her forward into the hall. Toward his past and all the skeletons that hid there.

EIGHT

Lydia faced a wall with an unidentified abstract painting hanging on it. She squinted to read its title on the card below, but without her glasses the letters all merged together.

"Lovely. Just lovely," came a man's voice from beside her.

She straightened to attention. "Really? You think it's lovely? I can't even tell what it is."

"Well, to be honest, I don't know what it is, either," the man responded with a deep chuckle. "You care to take a guess?"

Lydia eyed the painting with her better eye. "Let's see, how about a DNA double helix?" She cringed. Why did her mind always go to science? If she could see the guy clearly, his eyes were probably glazed over already.

"Interesting. I was going to say a spiral-like structure that looks like a twisted ladder."

"Yeah, that, too. Sorry. I'm an anthropologist. You can take the girl out of the lab, but you can't take the lab out of the girl."

He laughed again. "An anthropologist. Sounds...exciting?"

"What you meant to say is boring and tedious, right?"

A woman server dressed in black and white and balancing a tray of fluted glasses passed by. The man snaked out a hand for a glass. "How about some champagne?" He avoided Lydia's question with ease.

"No, thank you." She smiled. "So, tell me, what did you think was so lovely about this painting? Do ladders thrill you for some reason?"

He peered over his glass. "Actually, I wasn't speaking about the painting."

Heat flushed Lydia's cheeks as her breath caught in her throat. The man was talking about *her?*

"I was noticing your ruby pendant. It looks quite rare."

The flush turned to a scorcher of embarrassment. "Oh, oh, yes, it is." Her hand went to her throat, where her fingers toyed with the piece that was lovelier than her. "I don't really know how rare, though."

"Did you buy it at auction?" He leaned in, raising his hand to shield his next words. "Or black market?"

An uneasy feeling made her squirm and take a step away. "It's not mine. It's on loan to me right now."

He pulled back, a shocked look spreading over his clean but imperfect face. A faint scar lined his right cheek. "Really?" he said. "I have to admit that would be a hard treasure to give back. The unique color of the stone tells me it's of the highest quality. It must be worth a million dollars if not more."

"A million dollars?" Had the woman it was buried with known the value? If she had swallowed it, then most likely yes? Had she swallowed it to protect it, only to get herself killed for it? But from whom?

"Everything all right here?" Wesley, the bulldog, was back. His stance and tone of voice caught her off guard. *Now* what was he mad about?

Lydia studied the territorial look in his eyes.

The man wasn't even on Stepping Stones. What was he protecting now?

"Certainly," the man answered. "Why wouldn't it be? We were only having a little chat."

A little chat. Lydia smiled outside and within. She *was* chatting, and doing fine.

Wesley reached for her arm and tugged her closer to him. Lydia looked down at his hand, then back to his hard face.

Her? He was protecting *her?*

Or did he keep her close because he didn't trust what she might say? She wanted to state she was quite capable of keeping them under the radar.

"Aren't you Wes Grant?" the man asked.

Wesley squinted until recognition crossed his face. "Brian O'Connor. We used to work together in campus security, right?"

"That's correct. I'm the head of the department now."

Wesley nodded without felicitations. "Are you working tonight? Or is this a personal evening?"

"I'm on duty. Mr. Carmichael likes for his security to dress for the occasion, which explains my tux. It makes his guests more comfortable. Plus, it makes for hidden eyes in the crowd should something get…lifted. He's learned his lesson in the past to always be watching. Which reminds me, didn't I escort you off the premises the last time you were here?"

"I left voluntarily. I did nothing wrong." Wesley's jaw ticked.

"Right. Well, if you'll excuse me, I need to get back to my job of always watching." The man nodded to Lydia with a now-creepy smile that halted her own. He turned away and dispersed into the crowds.

"I take it he wasn't a friend." Lydia broke the silence hanging between them.

"Stay away from him," Wesley warned and left her side without another word.

She gripped her upper arms feeling tainted as though she'd done something wrong. Even though she hadn't, Wesley believed she would given the opportunity.

He really didn't trust her, and Lydia began to think he never would.

Her throat felt dry and raw. She pushed

through the crowd to find a glass of water. Everywhere she looked through her blurred vision, she caught people looking at her. One by one, she ignored their stares and moved through the crowd until she spotted a wait-ress with water glasses.

Her steps picked up, and she snatched up a glass. Just as the refreshing water touched her tight and dried lips, a hand grabbed her wrist, spilling the contents down her dress.

"Who did you kill to get that?"

"Excuse me?" Lydia snapped her head up from her soaked dress to find Dr. Simon Webber standing before her, his shock of crazy white hair messier than usual. "Dr. Webber?" Lydia pulled her arm away and searched quickly through the blurred crowd for Wesley. She spotted him and thought he was watching her over his water glass. He was probably jealous of Webber now. Lydia turned her back to him. "What are you doing here?" she asked her boss.

"*That* is a question for *you* to answer," Dr. Webber said in his nasally voice. "Imagine my surprise when I received a phone call from the Carmichaels that one of my own employees was investigating a crime and bothering the good people of Boston. I said, 'No, it couldn't be one of mine. My anthropologists follow my orders.' And I believe the orders I gave you, Miss Muir, were to bring the remains back to the lab where I would determine if an investigation was in order."

"You don't understand. Someone stole the skull. I had to look for other evidence to—"

"You lost the skull?" Dr. Webber pulled her back through a curtained alcove. His voice dropped to a harsh whisper. "Why am I just hearing about this?"

"I was planning on telling you, but I thought I might be able to find other ways to identify the woman before I contacted you."

"By parading around in a slave-trade ruby? FYI, they don't call them blood rubies because of their color."

"Slave trade?" Lydia touched the ruby at her neck, burning more now than ever before. The image of children clawing away at earth and stone in search of gems for a warlord standing over them came to mind—and sickened her stomach.

"Come with me." Dr. Webber led her blindly into a dark corridor. After multiple lefts and rights, she realized she had no idea where he was taking her or how she would find her way back.

Then he squeezed her arm and pulled harder, making her wonder if she should be with Dr. Webber at all. Especially when their steps led them to darker places.

Wesley's warning came back loud and clear. *"Bad things happen in dark places."*

Wesley circled back around from searching the whole area for the third time. Carmichael was nowhere to be found. The man had yet to arrive to his own event. What was so important that he would miss this opportunity to plume his feathers in front of all his followers?

There was the possibility the man already knew about their visit to his house earlier from the missus. But if that was the case,

Carmichael would have had the Boston police here waiting for him, ready for another fight.

But so far, the only hostility Wesley had to contend with was with his lady in red.

He shot a look to the spot where Lydia had been speaking to that crazy-haired man before. But they were gone. Some different men in tuxes conversed there now. A 360-degree scan took him around with no sight of her.

"Who's the woman in the red dress, and where did she get that stone? That's what I want to know."

Wesley skidded to a stop at the dripping venom drifting his way. An elderly couple was gossiping about Lydia.

"She's our thief. I inspect and catalogue everything that comes into this museum, and I remember that stone clearly."

"That jewel came in with the House of Bonaparte Collection. We lost millions when pieces of it were stolen. What that little thief did to our credibility as a museum is deplorable. I could rip her eyes out."

The House of Bonaparte Collection. Stolen pieces. Wesley squeezed his eyes shut as the words found meaning in the recesses of his mind.

Those were the pieces stolen on my watch, and why I was fired.

If the ruby was part of that collection, then he had his answer. Jenny did get him fired, after all. Had *she* stolen it when she cried someone was following her and he'd ran off to inspect the area? Or was she holding it for the person who did? Was she killed for it?

If so, would the person kill again for it? Like his lady in red wearing it now?

Lydia.

Wesley's bow tie tightened around his neck as he scanned through the crowds for her. Back and forth his gaze roamed. At her height, she should be a head above all of them—and she was, in more ways than height.

"Did you lose your girlfriend already?"

Wesley whipped around to find Brian O'Connor standing there. "Did you see her leave?" he asked in a rush, remembering how she turned her back on him the last time he saw her.

The weasel laughed and took a slow sip of

his champagne. His tongue flicked a leftover droplet from the corner of his lips, dragging out his response. "Like I said. I'm paid to watch."

"Where'd she go?"

"I'm actually not at all surprised she left you. Jenny got tired of being a pauper real fast, too."

Wesley cut him a sharp glance. "What do you know about Jenny?"

"Now, don't worry, Wes. Your secret's safe with me."

"And what secret would that be?" A step closer dared the man to continue.

O'Connor didn't flinch. "That you're worthless, and you've got nothing to offer a lady but a life of misery." He checked his watch. "It didn't take the pretty lady long to figure it out. Not long at all."

Fighting this man was not an option. At least not here. Wesley rejected O'Connor and took the back exit. When he reached the shadows of a long stone corridor, he leaned a hand on a smooth marble pillar, realizing his heart was racing. The cool surface seeped in to simmer down what O'Connor's obvious statement boiled up.

Wesley had nothing to offer a woman. He also had no business putting himself out there to be trampled on again. The fact that Lydia left him behind tonight without even a good-bye proved he was right in his vow to go it solo.

First Jenny, now Lydia.

Wesley shook his head and grabbed his new replacement cell phone from his tux pocket. He'd picked it up this afternoon after he cut his hair to make the woman smile.

Disgusted with himself, he dialed Charlie.

The chauffeur picked up immediately. "Are you ready to leave, Sheriff?"

"Actually, I'm calling to tell you I won't be joining Lydia. You can take her home."

"Lydia? I don't have Lydia with me. Isn't she with you?" Charlie's voice rose with a little panic. "Sir, please tell me you're keeping an eye out for her."

Wesley stood silently in the dark corridor. The darkness seemed to creep closer toward him, reminding him of the message he gave Lydia earlier.

Bad things happen in dark places.

How quickly he let his pride make him forget.

Wesley clicked the *End Call* button and ran straight into the darkness with one goal in mind. Find Lydia before his message came true.

"You have a lot of explaining to do, Miss Muir. And you're going to explain it to Mr. Carmichael directly." Dr. Simon Webber held fast to Lydia's forearm. He hauled her through a maze of dark antiquated halls that blended from one to another. She wished for a spool of thread running from the main hall. A guarantee of her return when she rewound it. At the rate of these turns, she'd never find her way back.

She really wished she'd stayed with Wesley. She wanted him to trust her so she could help him, but leaving him without a word wouldn't earn her bonus points. "Where are we going? You said it wasn't far." She yanked her arm from the grasp of her infuriating boss as they approached a room, light spilling out into the dark corridor.

"I'm taking you to Mr. Carmichael so you can personally apologize for upsetting his wife today."

"Upsetting *her?* I will not apologize. It's them who should apologize for—"

"Is this the woman who came to my home?" A man at the lit doorway cut her off.

"Yes, Mr. Carmichael, this is Lydia Muir, one of my soon-to-be ex-anthropologists. She—"

"Muir, you say. Any relation to Dr. Gerard Muir?"

Lydia straightened away from Dr. Webber. "Yes, I'm his daughter."

"Estelle," Carmichael called over his shoulder. "Did you hear this? Dr. Gerard Muir is her father."

"I *knew* I recognized the name." The woman Lydia met earlier today appeared beside her husband. "Come in, Dr. Muir. If I had known, I would have been more open to speaking with you earlier."

"I don't see how my father makes me more credible."

"Well, dear, your father is a dean at the university. He's a very accomplished scientist. In fact, wasn't he one of your students before you retired from teaching, Dr. Webber?"

Dr. Webber nodded but kept his face blank.

"Seriously?" Lydia looked to Dr. Webber. "You were my father's teacher?"

Estelle reached for Lydia's hands. "So you see, dear, you're one of us." Her refined face twisted to revulsion. "Except, when you came to my home with the likes of Wesley Grant, it was hard to tell."

"Speaking of Wesley Grant," Mr. Carmichael cut in. "Why are you traveling with him? He is a thief and could be dangerous. I have to think your father would be very concerned for your safety."

"I make my own decisions, and about Wesley being a thief, he believes he was framed."

"Of course he would say that. He wouldn't exactly incriminate himself, now, would he? Please tell me hearsay isn't how you conduct your cases. Please tell me you base your findings on evidence."

"Always, and that includes the lack of. I won't assume Wesley is guilty unless I have evidence that points me in that direction. If he stole the jewelry, what would he do with it? I don't see evidence that he sold it. He's not exactly living the high life—" Lydia stopped because both Estelle and Calvin were ogling the ruby at her neck.

Speaking of jewelry...

"Do you recognize it?" Lydia asked.

Calvin looked to Webber and back to Lydia. He met her eyes this time. "My dear, that stone is tainted. Wherever did you get it?"

"It was found with a skeleton on Stepping Stones Island. I believe it will lead me to the identification of the woman."

"The only thing it will lead you to is danger. You're bound to attract the wrong sort of people wearing that."

"They're the people I want to attract so justice can be served. And whether you believe it or not, that's what Wesley wants, too. Will you come with me to talk with him?"

"I owe that man nothing. He took my daughter away from me. The only joy I can take from the whole thing is that Jennifer and I parted on good terms. A few weeks before Jennifer decided to leave the island, she called to tell us she was leaving Grant for someone else. Someone we could approve of. He had a yacht and would be coming to get her. We were ecstatic and told her all was forgiven. And to come home." Calvin frowned on a sigh. "That was the last we heard from her."

Lydia grew silent for a moment. She had questions that needed to be answered, regardless of their pain over the loss of their daughter. *Empathy, Lydia, empathy.* She opened her mouth slowly to tread carefully. "Mr. Carmichael, you believe your daughter drowned in the Mediterranean. Can I ask why?"

"The authorities in Malta contacted us. A woman fitting her description fell overboard at sea. The yacht belonged to her new husband. We have no reason to believe it wasn't her. Why? Do you?"

"Reason? Yes. Evidence? No. All I know is I have unidentified remains that belonged to a woman between twenty-five and thirty years old. They were buried less than ten years ago. I believe they belong to your daughter."

Calvin's eyes glittered with unshed tears and excitement. "Well, let's identify them, then. What do you need? Her dental records? I can get them to you tomorrow."

"I appreciate your assistance, and I will take them. Send them to Dr. Webber's office."

"Yes," Dr. Webber intruded. "Send them to me, because I will be taking over this case. What she's not telling you is she's lost the skull."

"Lost? You've lost my Jennifer's skull? Are you saying we've found her only to lose her again?"

Lydia took a step closer. "This is why it's important that you come and speak with Wesley, Mr. Carmichael. We're working to find it, but we need everyone's help...regardless of bad blood."

"No, Calvin," Estelle said when her husband nodded and stepped to the door. "Do not help that man."

"Dr. Webber, please stay with my wife. Estelle, I need to do this for Jennifer." He waved a hand for Lydia to exit back into the dark corridor before him.

She took the steps a little easier this time, grateful for the guide through the long halls. They took about three turns through the corridors before he stopped abruptly. "Oh, please forgive my absent-mindedness. I've forgotten something I need for the gala. Would you mind waiting one moment while I rush back?"

Did she mind? Yes, but the man didn't wait for an answer. He quickly retraced his steps until she no longer heard the echoing tap of his shoes on the marble floors and off the tall walls that made her actually feel small.

She chuckled nervously. It wasn't too often she could refer to herself as small.

Time extended into minutes. Too many minutes. Lydia sighed and looked down the hall he had retreated to. He didn't appear to be coming back. Lydia gripped her elbows to ward off a chill of nerves. Wesley's warning echoed in her head. Bad things could happen in these dark, shadowed halls. What kinds of bad things? she wondered, but she didn't want to find out.

Waiting for Carmichael ended now.

Her tapping heels picked up a steady cadence as she set out through one hall, then down another. The tattoo slowed a bit before she came to a stop with nothing but silence and tall marbled columns around her. Had she been down this hall before? Darkened corners and crevices drew her attention and reminded her again.

Bad things.

She turned back to the last juncture and took a right instead. Immediately, Lydia noticed another intersection of halls looming ahead. Dread filled her as she contemplated yet another unknown path of choice.

Long-standing portraits lined the walls. Ancient eyes seemed to shift as she moved past feeling like a dead woman walking. Rembrandt's *Night Watch* with painted men wearing Old Dutch garb and drawing their bayonets on her, tracked her every step. The famous painting apparently on loan from the Rijksmuseum in Amsterdam had never affected her so gravely before.

Lydia rushed past it. It's only a painting, she reassured herself. *It's not hunting you.*

She reached the end of the hall and took a fast right. More terrifying darkness enveloped her. Another wrong choice that took her farther away from where she wanted to be. Farther away from the light...and Wesley.

Lydia pivoted on her heel to go back, but before she took another step, pain exploded at her throat. Her hands went to her throat as a severe force yanked her back by the chain around her neck. Searing pain bit into her skin, cutting off her air supply and leaving her grappling for her life. She fumbled at her neck where the necklace held fast and tight against her skin. Thin, shaking fingers pried at the gold strand but gained no access in between it and her battered flesh.

She opened her mouth to scream, but only strangled tones escaped her. Her body was pulled straight back. Not down, but back. Did that mean her assailant was the same height as her? The thought sprang to her mind amidst the chaos of suffocation.

She had moments to live—another fact clear in her head. Seconds to free herself or die by strangulation.

Lydia flung her frame back, using the element of surprise. As her body collided with a man's hard chest, she raised her heel to stomp on his instep.

He grunted, and for one brief second her chain loosened enough to allow her to slip a finger in and attempt a scream. To her ears, it sounded pitiful and useless. She doubted it echoed through this hall, never mind down the others.

Before she could twist away, the man firmed up his choke hold on her again and all thoughts but finding air vanished. The one fingertip to take some of the pressure off her airway wasn't enough to fill her lungs. They burned to a molten heat as the final prolonged torturous pain overtook her.

Black spots darker than the hall's secret hiding places loomed above her eyes as Wesley's warning came true. Bad things do happen in dark places.

Wesley strained to hear, but since that one tiny squeak, he hadn't heard a thing. He wasn't even sure the squeak was anything to worry about. Could have been a sneaker tread on the marble floors. Could have been mice fighting over a dropped lobster-in-blanket thingy the waiters were serving. All he could do was move forward in the direction he thought the sound came from.

God, are You with me right now? Lydia believes You're still my guide even though I don't. Is she right? Are You still with me?

No answer came. No feeling of any presence accompanied him in this long stone hallway.

"I guess I'm not surprised," Wesley muttered. He had to think Lydia was crazy for putting her trust in something that lacked evidence. What kind of scientist was she if she could forgo the facts in front of her for blind faith?

And yet he continued to walk blindly down a hall because of a squeak he might or might not have heard.

His steps stayed straight. An old scripture resurfaced in his mind. One of the many Proverbs his mom used to recite when he was young. They still floated around in his brain as useless information. *"Seek God in all you do,"* she would tell him, *"and He will make your paths straight."*

But then she died, so after all that, she could keep her Proverbs. Wesley just wished he could get them out of his head.

The juncture of another hall approached. The dark quiet said Lydia wasn't down this wing. His common sense said turn back, but his feet weren't following his common sense. They continued forward, walking on farther down the hall until a sound caught his ear.

He craned his head to the right. A whimper, maybe? A scuffle? He turned the corner and caught the silhouette of two people struggling in a ray of moonlight.

One wore a dress and looked to be grabbing at her throat.

"Let her go!" Wesley cranked up his speed, but the person in the rear threw the woman forward and disappeared into one of the dark arches. The man's shoes tapped out his quick getaway, luring Wesley to chase him down. To identify this assailant and make him pay for hurting the gagging woman on the floor.

He didn't need a light to know the woman was Lydia.

"I need help down here!" he yelled over his shoulder, running up to her and dropping to his knees. He gave up peering after the escapee to give his full attention to Lydia. He pulled her convulsive frame into his arms and removed her hands from where they grabbed at her neck.

Blood dripped from a thin line that could only have been made by the chain still secured there. The guy had been after Jenny's ruby. And willing to kill for it. Or perhaps kill again for it.

Lydia whimpered in Wesley's arms. Her mouth moved, but nothing but painful whimpers leaked out. Each sound of raw agony felt like torture, but he would gladly take all her pain if he could.

"Shh, don't try to talk." He leaned in, touching her forehead to his. "You're safe now. I won't let anyone hurt you again. I'm sorry I got you into this mess. I should have realized anything with Jenny's name attached to it would be a nightmare."

Footsteps raced up behind Wesley. "What happened?" a man asked, and Wesley looked up at the man he'd been waiting to speak to all night.

Calvin Carmichael.

Wesley's voice rumbled at the man with suppressed rage. "Your daughter happened, that's what. It appears she's still causing chaos from whatever grave she's in."

A vacuum of voices spoke above Lydia. Her eyes scrunched closed to dull the burning in her lungs and at her throat. Would it ever subside? She forced herself to take another slow, deep breath from her prostrate position on the floor.

"That's it, breathe in and out. I've got you. You're safe. Just breathe. Please breathe." Wesley's voice cracked as he tightened his arms around her.

Lydia relaxed in his hold, knowing this was the true man behind the gruff exterior. The one he kept hidden from the world, for fear of being shamed and rejected again. And what had she done in her weak, prideful moment?

Turned her back on him when she could have shown him understanding and mercy. *Lord, forgive me. Show me how I can help him.*

Lydia pushed passed the pain to open her eyes, but instead of looking at Wesley, her gaze caught on the man peering over his shoulder.

Calvin Carmichael.

"Dr. Muir, did you see the person who hurt you?" Carmichael asked. His wife wrung her hands on one side of him. Brian O'Connor stood on the other.

Lydia shook her head in answer to his question. Her lips moved to say no, but only a croak slipped out. All she could remember from the attack was thinking her assailant matched her height.

She grabbed at the ruby still resting at her clavicle. Still attached to her. Because of Wesley.

Lydia focused on him only. She reached a hand to his face. His rigid, clean-shaven cheek filled her palm. She felt his jaw tick and knew his teeth were clenched in their normal state of torture. But instead of anger in his eyes, worry flared. Worry for her? Did he know she worried for him?

She rubbed gently along his jawbone. With each sweep of her thumb, he let go of the tension.

"I'm okay," she pushed out on a whisper. His shoulders slumped for a moment on his exhale of relief.

But only for a moment.

"I'm getting you out of here," he announced, and swept her up in his arms as he stood. Lydia let her head rest on his chest, the rapid beat of his heart thrumming against her ear.

"I won't let you take her." Mrs. Carmichael jumped in his way. "Not when it was probably you who hurt her. Just like you hurt Jennifer."

"Think what you want. All I care about is getting Lydia to a safe place. Now move out of my way."

"She can rest at our home. I'll bring a doctor in."

"Not a chance. You're the people I need to protect her from."

A blockade of Mr. and Mrs. Carmichael

and their security piled in. Lydia had to say something before Wesley found himself in either handcuffs or fisticuffs. She raised a hand to halt anyone from coming closer. "I want to go home," she whispered past the pain. "My father's chauffeur is here and will take me to his house."

Brian O'Connor stepped in. "I'll accompany them to the car to make sure, Mrs. Carmichael."

Estelle's lips pinched, but at her sidestep, Wesley rushed past, carrying Lydia to the only place she wanted to be.

Home.

NINE

Wesley pressed his cheek onto Lydia's silky hair. They sat in silence, clutched together in the rear seat of the car. He hadn't released her since he'd scooped her up in the hall, and now he tucked her head into the crook of his neck even closer. His fingers played in her loosened strands of hair, while hers gripped his wrist with the same desperation he felt.

He told himself it was only because she'd nearly been taken from this world three times today, but that didn't explain the ache in his chest that went beyond guilt. That didn't explain how perfectly she filled his arms and his need to never let her go.

"We're almost there," she whispered. She lifted her face to him. Lights from passing cars moved across her pale skin, revealing a haunted look in her eyes.

Wesley felt his gut twist, knowing it was there because of him. She would probably have nightmares for the rest of her life after the events of today.

"Wesley, there's something I need to tell you before we get there." She swallowed hard and Wesley noticed a flinch of pain behind her mask of bravery.

He pushed a hanging tendril behind her ear. His finger fell to her soft lips. "We'll talk tomorrow. Close your eyes and rest. We'll be there soon. Charlie made sure a doctor would be waiting." He smirked. "I have to admit, I'm impressed. Not too many doctors perform house calls these days. Your dad must have some friends in high places."

Lydia turned away to the window without a response and after a few minutes, she let her eyelids shutter closed. Her head fell back onto his shoulder as exhaustion from her tumultuous day won over. After a few more minutes the car took a right and stopped.

An iron gate loomed in front of them.

"Is everything all right, Charlie?" Wesley asked quietly, not to rouse Lydia.

"Everything's fine, sir. We're here."

"Here? Where's here?"

The iron gates opened onto a long paved road. "Home," Charlie answered, and drove the car down the narrow road. Wide oak trees lined and canopied the route, leading up to an enormous Colonial mansion lit in preparation of their arrival.

No, not their arrival. Lydia's arrival. As Charlie had said, this was her home.

Wesley sat dumbstruck as the car took the wide half-circle driveway to the front entrance. Two doors were pulled wide by a man in a suit. The lit foyer behind him showed rich red carpeted stairs that a tall, bald man rushed down.

He sped out the front door and reached the car in record time, opening the door before Charlie could perform his routine duties. The bald man ignored Wesley and held his arms out for Lydia to be passed over. "Give me my daughter."

"She's sleeping. I'll carry her in," Wesley said, not ready to let her go—even if she apparently *was* royalty and he had no business holding her.

The man whispered out rushed directions and led him up the red stairs and down a hall of gold, gilded frames containing pictures of people who looked as though they belonged to another era.

With each Muir family ancestor Wesley passed, and with each step to her four-poster bed, set in a bedroom the size of his whole house, Wesley realized Lydia Muir was more out of his league than Jenny ever was.

A short, stocky doctor waited in the room and took over as soon as Wesley laid her down. The man unclasped the necklace so he could inspect the wounds, then passed the necklace over to Wesley. Elongated moments transpired while the swaying ruby made him recoil as though it were last week's garbage covered with maggots. The only good thing was that the offensive thing was finally off Lydia's neck.

He snatched the piece and shoved it into the pocket of his tux without another look.

"Let's leave the doctor to his job, shall we?"

Lydia's father said, and gestured for Wesley to leave the room.

At the soft click of the door closing, Wesley stood paralyzed on the lush carpeted hallway.

"Looks like you might need the doctor, too," her father said. "Perhaps you want to sit down before you fall down."

Wesley backed up to some sort of couch. Or was it called a settee? Whatever it was dubbed, he dropped down into it, feeling the smooth fabric against his fingers as his hands curled around the seat's edge. The piece probably cost more than all his furniture combined.

"Better?" the man asked.

"Not really," Wesley mumbled, his stomach capsized.

"Well, too bad." The man folded his arms at his chest. Nausea would have to wait until Daddy Warbucks said his piece. "I want an explanation of why you are traipsing my daughter across state lines and putting her life at risk. Let's hear it, Sheriff. What's your excuse for nearly getting my daughter killed?"

Wesley shrugged. "That's easy. I'm worthless, and I have nothing to offer a lady but a life of misery."

Lydia's father remained still and quiet.

"How much do you value your daughter's life?" Wesley asked.

"More than anything in this world."

"Then you might want to ask me to leave, because I'm nothing but poison to her." Wesley jutted his chin toward the white bedroom door. "As you can see."

The man rubbed a hand over his smooth, shiny head and sighed deep. "My first inclination is to do just that."

"So what are you waiting for?"

Lydia's father came and sat beside him. "To be honest, I'm kind of afraid to. My daughter is… Let's just say she's strong-willed and likes to express her own mind."

Wesley felt his lips crack into a short laugh. "So I've noticed."

An image of Lydia going head-to-head with him above the skeleton at their feet flashed in his mind. He smiled a little bigger. Then he thought of her screeching about him flying the helicopter, and his smile became an all-out laugh.

Until he remembered the fear in her eyes when he told her they were going down.

Wesley dropped his head into his hands. His head shook back and forth over the danger he'd put her in today. "I'm sorry. I know my apology isn't worth anything, but I *am* sorry. It was my job to watch over her, and I messed up."

"Your job? I can see why you might think that, but I'm pretty sure Lydia would object. She knows Who has her back and Who's gone before her to pave the way."

"Right. Her guide as she puts it."

"You don't believe her?"

"Let's just say tonight, when I asked God to help me find her, all I was met with was silence."

"I'm not following… You found her, didn't you?"

"Yes, but—"

"But you were expecting a lightning bolt. Something that said the mighty God bestows

His presence on you. You were looking for physical evidence?"

Wesley angled a look at Lydia's father. "I wasn't looking for a lightning bolt...just a feeling."

"What kind of feeling?"

Wesley shook his head. "I don't know. That's the problem." He jumped to his feet and paced to Lydia's door. He stopped and wished he had X-ray vision to see through the thick wood. He imagined her face before she was hurt. When she was safe and content to be digging in the dirt. "Whatever the feeling is, she has it. I've seen it in her eyes. On her face, especially when she's working. It's beautiful. It's..."

"Peace."

Wesley whipped around. "Yes. Peace."

The older man's serious face slowly relaxed into a slight smile. "Well, Sheriff Grant, regardless that you've caused my daughter to fight for her life today, I owe you my gratitude."

"Gratitude? Did you not hear me? Poison.

You're a scientist. You do know what poison is, right? What it does to a person?"

"I'm fully aware, but if what you've seen is true, that you've witnessed peace in my daughter, then you have given me a great gift." Dr. Muir folded his hands loosely in his lap. His head dropped down as he seemed to let the stress of the evening go on a deep sigh. "I did my best to be a good father, teaching her everything I knew. I never held anything back. She was a sponge and my best student. But no matter what I taught her or what I said, she still felt inadequate. When we're in the same room together, I don't see peace. I see a girl who thinks she has to compete with my so-called legacy."

"She's brilliant," Wesley said.

"Yes, she is. She's a capable, intelligent and virtuous woman."

Wesley searched his mind, blindly looking to the decorative ceiling and gold light fixture hanging from the ceiling. "Let's see, that's Proverbs 31, right?"

The older man smiled. "I'm happy to see you know your scripture. But do you know what it says about the man who can find such a woman?"

Wesley held his tongue for a few seconds before answering "Yeah. My mom quoted this one by heart. The scripture says he's someone who trusts in her."

Lydia's father nodded, and in all seriousness asked, "Are you that man, Sheriff?"

The door opened behind Wesley, saving him from answering and causing him to swing around. The physician exited the door and shut it on a quiet click. "Is she okay?" Wesley pushed out, his voice gravelly.

The man looked to Lydia's father, who stepped up beside Wesley. "May I share freely, Gerard?" The question was meant for permission to speak in front of Wesley. After all, he wasn't family. He wasn't anything to her.

"This is Wesley Grant, a friend of Lydia's. It's okay to speak to him. Wesley, this is Dr. Segal."

Saying it was nice to meet the man didn't feel right. He settled for saying, "Thank you for helping her." The doctor unrolled his cuffs to refasten the buttons. He looked as though he'd come from his own spiffy event tonight. Come to help Lydia. "I didn't know doctors still made house calls."

Gerard chuckled. "He's gone further than that in his career and for God. We met years ago overseas when he was there for a mission tour with Doctors Without Borders. We've volunteered for many more missions together since."

Dr. Segal nodded firmly. "I just go when God tells me to. Gerard and I have been blessed financially and intellectually. If God can use us, we go and share what He has given to us."

The two men locked eyes; then Gerard asked, "How's Lydia?"

A reassuring smile crossed Dr. Segal's face. "She's sleeping now, but there's nothing to worry about. She'll be fine. She'll have some soreness and obviously the external cuts and abrasions will need to heal, but her breathing sounds good. I'll stay tonight to observe just in case." He looked to Wesley. "May I see the necklace she wore?"

"The necklace?" The question caught him off guard, but Wesley reached into his pocket and brought it back out. He handed it over without looking at it.

Dr. Segal lifted it to the light. "Pigeon's blood. Don't you think, Gerard?"

"You can't be serious." Gerard stepped closer to the light to study the piece. His head jerked with accusing eyes at Wesley. "Why is my daughter wearing this filthy thing?"

Wesley hesitated to answer, not sure where this conversation was headed. "I take it you know something about this stone?"

"Do you?"

"Not a clue. It was found with a skeleton we were investigating on Stepping Stones Island. We're trying to put the pieces together. What can you tell me?"

The two doctors looked at each other with heated concern. Gerard turned back. "We've done a few missions to Thailand. These gems come from a nearby country."

"How can you tell?"

"Rubies actually vary in color because the pure corundum that forms them is colorless.

They get their color from the level of chromium in the land, and the land this came from is the only place on Earth that produces a ruby the color of pigeon's blood. They're the most expensive gems per carat in the world. I can't tell you the price of this stone, only that the child who dug for it with his bare hands didn't make a penny."

Wesley's mouth dropped. "Slave labor."

"Dangerous slave labor. I can also tell you, no one bought this gem in their local jewelry store. Trading is banned. So, how did your skeleton get it?"

"It doesn't matter. What matters is who killed her for it. Because whoever it is tried to kill Lydia today, and they won't stop until they succeed."

TEN

Male voices drifted to Lydia's ears from the dining room. The thick, carpeted stairs absorbed any sounds her footsteps made as she eavesdropped on the sense of mood between her father and Wesley. Through the open French doors, she could hear that the conversation sounded subdued but not unpleasant. Maybe she'd worried for nothing.

Last night, she'd wanted to warn Wesley about her home. She'd wanted him to know he was welcome here. She remembered being almost panicked in the car, worried the size of her home might make him think she was better than him. She knew after his visit to the Carmichaels' he might let something as silly as her bank account come between them.

Between them, as though there was actually something between them. She scoffed inwardly, but felt her lips tremble downward. She swallowed hard past the pain at her throat, her hand reaching to touch the bandage there, and felt the sting in her heart. None of it made sense.

God, I know You want to give me the desires of my heart, but I always believed that meant my career. What is this man to me? Is he just another step up in my career, or is he something more? Help me to see Your will clearly.

Lydia pushed the old extra pair of glasses she'd found in her bedside table back up on her nose. At the doorway she heard a cell phone ring in the room. When Wesley answered it, she realized he must have replaced his water-soaked one yesterday when she was getting her dress. She wished she had replaced hers.

"What's going on, Owen?" Wesley spoke into the phone, his tense voice caught her attention.

Lydia hesitated in the doorway, behind the backs of Wesley and her father.

"I'll be back in a few hours. Hold her."

Wesley jumped to his feet, pocketing his cell phone into his tux pants. He scooped up the black coat from the chair and stuffed his arms into the sleeves, bringing it up onto his broad shoulders.

"Duty calls, Dr. Muir. Hate to take off, but the evidence I need to solve this case just showed up."

"The skull?"

"Yup, some dog dragged it out of a neighbor's garage."

Lydia entered the room. "Whose?"

Both men swung around, startled to find her there. Her father got to his feet as Wesley answered, "Pat."

"Pat took the skull?" Lydia asked. "Why?"

"I don't know. I'll find out when I get there. I have to go right now. I'll call you—"

"You're leaving me?" Her voice squeaked as she strained to speak through the pain of her throat and her accelerating heartbeat.

"I planned on talking to you today about it, but I think it's best if someone else takes over the case." He approached the door, but Lydia blocked his path.

She felt herself grow flustered as panic and a jolt of hurt set in. "You don't think I can handle the case? Is that it? You doubt me?"

"You were nearly killed."

"That's not my fault."

"No, it was mine, and I won't let it happen again." He sidestepped her and entered the hallway.

She turned and spoke quickly to stop him. "I promised I'd keep Stepping Stones protected from the media. If I hand this case over, that promise is gone. Is that what you want, Sheriff? To bring the media onto your shores in droves? To bring chaos to the islanders' lives?"

Guilt swamped her, but she held his gaze steady. Deep down, she had to ask why she played that card. Was it because she couldn't pass the case over to someone else, or because the idea of leaving Wesley alarmed her?

He swallowed hard while he locked angry eyes on her bandaged throat. He gave a short shake to his head, while his jaw ticked viciously. Confliction marred his face, but he ground out, "I'm making flight plans. Be ready in twenty." He left her standing there with the blatant message that he wasn't happy with this outcome at all.

He wasn't happy, but she suddenly was able to breathe again. Again, she had to question why? She turned and faced the only other inhabitant in the room.

Her father. He looked like he was silently asking her the same question.

Faced with the decision to choose between her father's doctorate stare-down and pouring a glass of O.J., Lydia chose the juice. She walked to the sideboard and took a glass from the stacked pyramid and filled it. With her back to the great Gerard Muir, her fingers curled around the glass, then tightened to stop the liquid from sloshing over the sides. When she realized the juice swayed because her hands shook, Lydia placed the glass down with a hard clink.

"You're awfully quiet." She whipped around to find him reseated. "Don't you have some lecture to bestow on me?"

"Do you want a lecture?" He rested his elbows on the armrests of his chair.

"No, but that never stopped you before."

"How about a question then?"

Lydia crossed her arms, waiting for whatever he wanted to ask. Probably something that would trip her up and remind her she wasn't as smart as him.

"Do you love him?"

And there it was. She knew him so well. But surprise, Great and Powerful Dr. Muir, she had a ready answer. "No, I do not love him." A wave of sadness swept over her as the words lingered in her ears. "The man can't even trust me. He's just like everyone else."

"Everyone else? Like who?"

"Like Dr. Webber, and apparently you. Why didn't you ever tell me Dr. Webber was your professor?"

He frowned for a moment. "Not much to tell. I had him as a professor for my doctorate in medical anthropology. I learned a lot from him."

"So then why does he hate me?"

Her father sighed. "I'm sorry to hear this. I imagine it's because I won the Nobel and he didn't. I already held a Ph.D. in chemistry when I started my anthropology doctorate. An opportunity arose for a three-person team to develop multi-scale models for complex chemical systems. I was chosen to be part of the team over him. I know he was let down, but I didn't realize how much until he left teaching shortly thereafter. He said, with me there, he had nothing more to offer the school. Unfortunately, some people believe if they can't be the best at something, then they shouldn't bother. The fact is, we all have talents to offer this world, and God can use us right where we are. Even if it's not going to get us any prestigious awards. I suppose Dr. Webber thought he needed recognition for it to be worth his time."

Lydia looked above his head to the wall behind him. Why did it feel like her father was talking about her?

Gerard continued, "I'm sorry he's made your job difficult. I tried to tell you he might not be the person to work for, but…but you thought I wasn't happy for you. You thought I wasn't proud of you. So I kept quiet." Her father leaned forward. "Trinket—"

"Don't call me that. It's ridiculous. I'm over six feet tall, and nobody will ever take me seriously if you keep calling me that."

Gerard's mouth opened in silence. "I didn't know it upset you. Your mom started calling you that when you were young. She would say she wanted to carry you around in her pocket like a trinket. After she left us, I wanted to keep the things she did alive for you. I wasn't thinking you would interpret it as me not supporting you. Proof that you're really smarter than I am. Lydia, I have always been proud of you."

She held up a hand. "Can you repeat that?"

"I've always been so proud—"

"No, the other part. About me being smarter than you."

Gerard smirked and crossed his arms. "Fine, but only this once. After this, you're going to have to prove it by explaining the components of ecological stoichiometry."

"Bring it."

Gerard laughed out loud, shaking his head. "Always my biggest competitor. But something tells me you take a little joy in it."

She tilted her head. "I'm waiting."

"Okay, okay. My dear, lovely daughter, you surpass me with your intelligence tenfold. I know your time will come when you will be decorated with more honors than you have walls to hang them on. But, Lydia…" He grew serious. "None of those honors matter if they come before everything and everyone else. Trust me. There are days I want to trash all of mine. Especially when they stand in the way of my relationship with you. No honor or medal is worth losing the people you love. Ever."

Guilt swamped her as she stared into her father's sad eyes. She felt convicted of allowing his awards to do just as he said. Come between them. "Oh, Daddy, I'm so sorry." She stepped up to the table, a foot from him. She reached out to cover his hand on the armrest. "You've always been my greatest champion. Not my competitor. I'm sorry I forgot that. I don't want anything to come between us, either. It's just that I want to be so much like you."

Her father grabbed tightly to her hand and stood, engulfing her in his strong arms. "You humble me and honor me."

Lydia breathed his familiar woodsy scent of aftershave in and realized she'd been gone too long from him. In her drive for success, she'd pushed him out of her life. "I love you, Daddy."

"I love you so much, Tri— I mean, Lydia."

She squeezed away the tears forming behind her eyes. "It's okay. You can call me Trinket as long as no one else is in the room." She pulled away. "But please, whatever you do, don't trash your awards."

He chuckled. "As long as you promise me you'll be careful. There's something about this case you're working on that is raising more than a red flag. I'm having a hard time letting you go. Wesley seems like he takes his job seriously, but what do you really know about him?"

"I know he needs my help." She looked her father in the eyes, then smiled sweetly.

"And I know I'm exactly where God can use my talents."

Gerard chuckled again and leaned in to kiss the tip of her nose. "Touché. Then go with God, and I'll be praying for you."

ELEVEN

Lydia and Wesley crunched along the sea-shell walkway leading up to the Stepping Stones Sheriff's Station. She handed Wesley back his new phone. Unfortunately, she didn't have time to replace hers before they left. "Dr. Webber didn't answer, but I left him a message. I told him we're back on the island and the skull is waiting for us at the station. He'll probably show up here to take over as soon as he hears his voice mail. That should make you happy, huh?"

Wesley pocketed the phone in annoying silence. He'd been this way since they left that morning. She wished he would say something. Anything. They'd been through too much together to have it all end on acrimonious terms.

All because she had a mind of her own and refused to stay home. She should be the one upset. Not him.

She stopped him with a hand on his forearm. "Please talk to me."

The station door opened with Deputy Vaughn behind it. He halted at the sight of them.

Lydia gave Wesley's arm a squeeze. "We can't go in there like this. They'll know something is wrong."

"Something *is* wrong. You shouldn't be here. You should be home where you're safe from harm. Safe from me." Wesley clamped down on his back molars, and the silence returned. His heated gaze caused her to drop her arm back to her side.

"Why do I need to be safe from you? You would never hurt me."

"How can you be sure of that? You know nothing about me. You have no idea of what I'm capable of."

A troubling memory from Boston sprang to the front of her eyes. Wesley's revulsion when he saw the ruby around her neck.

She stepped away with uncertainty growing inside her. "Let's just get this skeleton identified, shall we?"

She passed through the door and tried her best to smile at Derek, but when she saw his eyes throwing malicious daggers at Wesley, a wave of concern for Wesley had Lydia nearly stepping in front of him as a shield.

Did Derek's hatred go beyond office discord? His threatening posture screamed *personal* and *deep-rooted*. But how deep-rooted? Since they were young kids on this small island? Did they fight over a girl in their teen years? Was the hatred strong enough to make Derek hurt Wesley? Strong enough to kill the woman Wesley once loved? Strong enough to make Derek cut the fuel line to the helicopter? Was it this man who nearly killed them? He *did* do the final checks before liftoff.

"Patty's in the back cell," Derek gruffly informed Wesley as he closed the door. "But I won't stand by and let you pin a murder on her. Not when the whole town knows the truth of who really killed Jenny."

* * *

"Why would you take the skull, Pat?" Wesley sat across from the disheveled young woman. Her red hair was so snarled and matted a seagull could mistake it for a nest.

She leaned in over the table separating them in the interview room and whispered, "I did it for you. So that doctor woman wouldn't be able to identify the skeleton. But then she said she could find out other ways, like by any clothes left behind." Pat picked repeatedly at the sleeve of her arm, nearly boring a hole through the fabric.

"Why don't you want her to find out who the skeleton is?"

"Because I know who it is."

Wesley sat with his back to the metallic-coated mirror. Lydia, Owen, Derek and Pat's father all stood behind the one-way glass. If Pat confessed to committing murder right now, this case would be closed. Pat would go to jail...and Lydia would go home.

Getting Lydia off his island should be a priority for her safety—and his peace of mind. But deep down, the idea of her leaving offered anything but peace. The thought of her leaving him behind nearly had him ending the interrogation and freeing Pat before she could say anything incriminating. Anything that would send Lydia on her way.

Even if that was the best thing for her.

Wesley focused on that and asked Pat the vital question. "How do you know who the skeleton is?"

Pat swallowed. "Because I put her there."

Hollering and banging from behind Wesley jolted him. In the next moment the door to the interrogation room flew wide, banging into the back wall with a crack. Derek trounced in, yelling, "Patty, don't say another word until I can get an attorney here."

Wesley bolted from his chair. "Derek, you are out of line. I've had enough of your violations. I don't care if I have no one to replace you. Clear out your desk and leave your badge and gun."

"So you can coerce her into admitting something she didn't do? Something that *you* actually did." Derek went head-to-toe with Wesley. "The whole island knows you killed Jenny."

Wesley flexed his fingers to keep from filling Derek's mouth with his fist, then turned away to get the answer he needed. "Pat, is the skeleton Jenny?"

Pat's lips trembled. Her face crumpled into a mess of flowing tears with a nod. "I buried her because I didn't want you to get into trouble. I couldn't let her body be found, or everyone would know."

"Know what?"

Derek flew to Pat's side. "Don't say another word. You may think you're helping him, but you're only digging your own grave."

"I didn't do anything wrong." Her eyes were only on Wesley. "I was helping you. Wesley, I love you. I've always loved you. Don't you know that? I couldn't let you go to jail for killing her. She didn't deserve you!"

"Did you kill Jenny?" Wesley's ears blared with Pat's piercing screeches while he restrained his own voice between gritted teeth. He couldn't believe this was how it would all go down. With Pat, the quirky girl next door, killing his fiancée. It felt so wrong. So sick.

"No!" Her hands slapped against the table. Her eyes filled with hysterics. "I didn't kill her. Why would you say that? How could you think that of me?"

"So you're saying you buried her, but you didn't kill her."

"Yes."

"You found her dead and thought burying her would be a good idea?" Sarcasm dripped before he could rein it back in.

"I didn't want you to go to jail."

"Why would I go to jail?" Wesley heard his yell and inhaled deeply to calm himself down.

"Because I found her at your house. She was lying in the sand down by your dock all cut up and…not breathing. I dragged her to the boat and was going to dump her, but I couldn't take the chance of her washing ashore. So I brought her to the rocky side of the island and I buried her. I thought it was deep enough, but it wasn't."

"You shouldn't have buried her, Pat.

Whether you killed her or not, I have to arrest you now."

"Arrest me? But I was helping you!"

"I didn't need your help, because I didn't kill her." The turning table of this interview shook him. Wesley breathed deep to gain control back over this cross-examination and to put it back onto Pat. "All you've done is allowed the real killer to go free. That's obstruction of justice. What were you thinking?"

"I was thinking about you, Wesley. I was thinking of how much she hurt you."

Wesley's stomach rolled. He turned to Owen. "Read her her rights. I need some air." Pushing past Owen and Lydia to get to the door, he felt the acid in his stomach churn to a molten concoction. He doubted he would make it to the rear exit in time.

Halfway down the hall Derek hollered, "Stop right there!" Before Wesley could turn around, the deputy rammed him in the back, sending him into the wall face-first. Blood spurted with the explosion of pain.

Nausea and now a bloody nose to contend with, Wesley grabbed at his face with one hand while the other attempted to block Derek's flying punch coming at him. The deputy found his target. Dead center into Wesley's solar plexus. A moment of paralysis bowled Wesley over for a few coughs, the wind knocked clean out of him. He came up. He brought his fists up with him, ready to take hold of the situation.

But the sight before him halted him in mid punch—and rocketed fear straight to his heart.

Lydia had stepped in front of Derek. Her height made it impossible for Wesley to get a lock on the man. Her hands raised high were a poor barrier. Her rail-thin body, a joke of a human shield. Even though she was a couple inches taller than Derek, she would be seriously injured if Derek laid a hand on her.

"Lydia," Wesley said carefully to the back of her head. He didn't miss the desperation threaded through his voice. "I need you to step away right now. You could get hurt."

"Listen to the man," Derek said, sneering.

"One girl is already dead. You better be careful, or you'll be next."

Derek shoved her with a force so strong she flew back. Wesley instantly wrapped her in his arms and shielded her with his body to keep Derek from touching her again. Over his shoulder he saw his ex-deputy escape out the back door.

"Are you okay?" Wesley spoke into Lydia's ear, protecting her in the cocoon of his arms.

She nodded as her breath hitched. She didn't try to extricate herself from his hold, and he took that as her needing a little more time to recover, too.

"Good. Now promise me you will never put yourself in harm's way like that again. He could have done a lot worse than shove you."

"I know." Her shoulders shook. "Wesley, I think he already might have."

He pressed his cheek alongside hers, breathing her in deep. "What do you mean?"

"He hates you. I see it in his eyes." She swallowed hard. "I think he was the one to cut the fuel line to the helicopter." Lydia tried to turn to face him, but Wesley tightened his hold. He looked back at the rear exit where Derek had disappeared. Wesley knew if he let go of Lydia right now, he would go after Derek and things would not end well for either of them.

If that man was responsible for nearly killing the woman in his arms, he would pay dearly for it.

With the skull cradled securely in one hand, Lydia scanned her handheld 3-D laser across the maxilla and mandible facial bones. As the slow and methodical red laser light passed over the teeth and jawline, the image on her laptop screen became complete. An exact replica of the skull in her hand stared back at her, waiting for the next step in the identification process.

This task involved layering the twenty-two bones of this human skull on the screen with virtual flesh in the hopes a name could be given to the real skeleton. The nose would take careful calculations and measurements of the cheek bones and lower forehead to give an accurate portrayal of the victim. Even then it wouldn't be perfect.

The eyes would be a guess, too. Lydia was glad she never saw a picture of Jenny. She wouldn't want her subconscious interfering with the outcome. Her product would be the result of her expertise and calculations alone.

The clack of her keyboard keys sped up as she wrapped the image of the cranium with layers of tissue and muscle followed by skin.

"How goes it?" Wesley asked from the doorway. He and Owen walked into the office space they'd given her to work in. A coffee appeared beside her on the table by Wesley's hand. "A little sugar. Just how you like it."

She smiled without removing her attention from the screen. "Thank you. I'm about to add some facial features and hair. Lips are first. Do you think she should smile?"

"Would you?"

"Good point."

Lydia worked on with the two men behind her quietly sipping their coffees and observing her every keystroke. Little by little the toothy grin of the wide, empty-eyed skull became a person. She gave the woman brown eyes and hair to her chin.

"Longer," Wesley said quietly over her shoulder. "Her hair went past her shoulders."

Lydia's hands stilled over the keyboard. "I take it you recognize her."

"The dental records will prove it, but I don't need them to be sure. What do you think, Owen?"

Owen's sigh expressed the strain they all felt in this pivotal moment. "I think I need to take over from here."

Lydia swiveled in her chair to catch Wesley's accepting nod. He was a suspect now. She expected to see his jaw tight with tension, but he looked surprisingly relaxed. Relaxed, but sad. She stood to face him, her hand reached out in front of her, but Wesley didn't take her offering of support and she let it fall to her side.

"I'll leave you two to discuss your course of action, whatever that may be." Wesley retreated, leaving her and Owen in a heavy silence.

The image of Jenny Carmichael on the

screen nearly caused Lydia to close it out. She hadn't meant to put a smile on the image, but the woman staring back at her wore a smirk that seemed to be a cruel, last-laugh dig.

"I don't believe Wesley killed her," Owen said.

Lydia studied the determined set to his jaw. If his best friend could stand by him without any doubts, maybe she could, too. "Okay. We better start looking for the evidence on the person who did, then. Because without it, Wesley will be the one to pay the price. And knowing the family Jenny came from, they'll be out for blood."

TWELVE

Lydia cut the engine of the police boat Owen lent her. The early morning sounds of the sea should have eased her nerves, but an unfamiliar boat lapped alone on the waves ahead.

Someone was at the dig site.

After anchoring her boat by a flat rock, Lydia grabbed her tool kit. With a click of its latches, she removed a scalpel and tucked the blade in the curve of her palm with its handle up her coat sleeve. After the recent attempts on her life, and with the attacker still being out there, she wasn't taking any chances.

There hadn't been a plan to come back out here, having already gone through the sand methodically before the Boston trip, but for Wesley's sake, another once-over was warranted. Every piece of clothing, every scrap of paper had already been numbered and tagged to identify the skeleton's identity. But maybe she missed something that would point to the identity of the killer.

Only she hadn't expected to find someone else snooping around out here and could only hope and pray it wasn't the killer.

Lydia left her kit for now. She stepped soundlessly on the flat rock with nothing but her hidden scalpel. A man's shoeprint led the way up and over the mound. If she crouched low she could peer over the mound without giving away her presence. She speculated the person had to have heard her boat come in, though. She didn't have the element of surprise on her side.

Calling out might be the best course of action before stepping too far from the safety of her boat. She opened her mouth to ask who was beyond the mound, but just as the first word formed on her lips, Wesley's voice carried from over it.

"It's only me, Lydia. You can put the weapon away. Although I am impressed that if you were fool enough to leave the safety of your boat, you didn't leave empty-handed."

A fleeting wave of relief exhaled from her lungs quickly followed by a deluge of furor. "You're calling me a fool, you fool!" Lydia stomped her way up through his sandy imprints. "How could you be so stupid as to come out to this site?" She came over the top to find him off to the side sitting on a large rock.

"Don't worry, Doc. I didn't touch anything. Besides, I've already been here enough times to leave any trace evidence."

He looked so forlorn sitting there all alone that the building anger rushed out of her faster than it had rushed in.

Then she saw the ruby, dangling from his palm.

Her feet sank in the soggy earth, glued to their spots, as her air seeped out of her lungs. "You shouldn't have that, Wesley. It's evidence."

He lifted his arm so the gem shimmered in the sun. "I always hated this thing. It hung on her neck, but really hung between us. A symbol of our different backgrounds. It would've never worked."

"If money is what you're basing it on, then you're right," Lydia said. "It never would have."

His gaze shot above the necklace to lock on hers. Slowly, he lowered the piece to his lap, his hand curled around it in a fist.

"It's more than that."

"Tell me. Please, Wesley, tell me."

Wesley looked down to the jewel, quiet for what felt like endless moments. Finally, he said, "I trusted her with everything. About my parents' deaths. About my dreams in law enforcement. About my love for her. But she—" He raised his gaze, shaking his head. "I didn't kill Jenny. I was hurt that she was leaving, but I didn't kill her."

"I know you didn't," Lydia's reply came swift and sounded so believable to her ears it stumped her for a moment. Perhaps because he finally confided in her, she could believe in him.

"You do?"

"Yes, but you need to leave so I can do another search around here. I need to look for something that might point me in the direction of who did, and your presence could skew my report."

"I would feel better if you weren't out here alone. Why isn't Owen with you?"

"Without you and Derek at the station, Owen's a one-man show. He can't go with me everywhere. Now I need you to leave."

"I don't like this. Too many dangerous things have happened, and I can't believe I'm saying this, but Stepping Stones may not be safe. I can't let another attempt on your life happen."

"Why, Wesley Grant, are you saying you would miss me?" She flashed a half smile at him.

"I'm saying this case goes deeper than a grave." He opened his palm, exposing the ruby. "This isn't your typical ruby."

"I know." She made the rest of the trek to stand in front of him, her palm out. He dropped the necklace into her hand, and she refastened it back on her neck. Until she could lock it up in her lab, the safest place for it would be on her person. "It was mined using slave labor and smuggled into the U.S."

Wesley's eyes narrowed on her before he gave a little laugh and shook his head. "I guess I shouldn't be surprised you figured it out. You would be the one person who could, but that also means you're smart enough to know not to walk around here alone with it around your neck. I don't want—" Wesley's cell phone rang. He unclipped it from his belt. "Grant here." After a few minutes of Wesley's silence, he ended the call and stood. "We gotta go. That was Owen." Wesley led the way over the mound. "Your boss just arrived in a rented boat. He's over at the station collecting all your evidence. Says he's here to take everything back to the lab. Come on." He grabbed her arm to move faster. "We've got to stop him. He can't do that to you. This is *your* case."

Lydia studied the back of this man who was ready to go to bat for her. Her heart swelled at his immediate response in her favor. Could it mean he finally believed in her? Or did he not want the evidence to get into the wrong hands because he was hiding something?

* * *

"Where's the ruby, Miss Muir?" Dr. Simon Webber's angry voice assaulted Wesley's ears before he reached the station's front door. "I don't appreciate you messing this case up by losing evidence."

Messing this case up? Before Wesley had both feet over the threshold, his blood boiled over. Who was this guy? How dare he speak to Lydia with such hostility?

Then Wesley saw the old man's pinched face and white hair and remembered him instantly. "This is the man I saw you with at the art gala." He didn't wait for confirmation. "Dr. Webber, is it? You're out of line. Dr. Muir has been nothing but professional. She's a good anthropologist and has done a fine job collecting and protecting the evidence in this case. She hasn't messed anything up."

Webber sputtered. "You! You shouldn't even be here. You're a suspect. Miss Muir, this is grounds for dismissal, never mind losing the promotion to director."

"Promotion?" Wesley looked to a blanch-faced Lydia. "What's he talking about?"

She shook her head. "It's nothing."

"Nothing? A promotion to director sounds like something to me. Why didn't you tell me?"

"Because there's nothing to tell." She faced Webber and unzipped her parka. "I haven't lost any evidence. See? I'm keeping it safe."

Wesley spoke under his breath. "It's not keeping *you* safe."

"He's right," Dr. Webber interjected. "I hate to admit it, but he's right. You should not be wearing it. Too many have put their lives in danger for that stone. The horrors are unspeakable. To lose you would be…" The old man grew flustered. He rubbed his forehead and looked down.

"Devastating?" Wesley finished for the man. "Heartbreaking? A waste?" Perhaps the two of them were on the same page after all. If they agreed on this, maybe Webber could be an ally for other things.

"Dr. Webber," Wesley asked. "I know I can't be involved with this case anymore, but could you share your opinion on how you think this stone entered the country. That's not a question directly related to the case, and it's just your opinion. If I was to hire you for your consulting expertise, what would you say?" At Simon's hesitation, Wesley threw in, "Off the record, of course."

The old man hummed in indecision for a moment, then said, "Well, by itself, the stone would raise a flag, but if it entered with a collection of other legit stones, it could slip by undetected."

"A collection?" The word triggered a past conversation. "Could it come through a museum collection?"

"I suppose. What kind?"

Wesley locked eyes on Lydia's as he said, "Perhaps a collection being passed off as the contents of some old aristocrat's jewelry box?"

"That would work," Simon speculated. "But collections on loan from other museums are strictly catalogued and protected. You might be able to get it in the country, but short of staging a grand theft larceny, you wouldn't get it out of the museum."

Wesley had yet to remove his gaze from

Lydia's. The frown on her face told him she already knew where he was headed. "Unless you've tricked the security guard into thinking he's in love with you."

She reached out for him, but he put his hands up to ward her off. His mixed bag of emotions collided inside him, and he didn't trust himself not to blow.

Now he knew what he always was to Jenny. Her patsy. She tricked him into believing someone was after her so he left his post long enough for her to steal the ruby.

Then used him again as a hideout until her man could come and get her.

Her man who she was probably working with to smuggle the gem in after obtaining it illegally…from dangerous, gun-toting slave drivers.

What had Jenny gotten herself into?

Wesley turned toward the door. He needed air. Now.

"Wesley." Lydia's urgent voice halted his footsteps. "I won't let you take the fall again."

"Go home, Lydia, before this whole thing destroys you. Please go home."

He opened the door and stepped out, but before the door closed behind him, he heard her giving Owen orders.

"I want everything on Jenny Carmichael in my hands now. I will solve this case if it kills me."

Wesley turned and watched her through the glass, struck by her strong will. Then he thought of the promotion she was trying to get. She said it was nothing, but a sickening feeling had him wondering if she was just like Jenny.

Was Lydia using him to get ahead, too?

THIRTEEN

"You shouldn't be here." Wesley scanned the darkness looming behind Lydia. She stood on his front porch with her laptop in front of her chest. "Where's Owen? Where's Webber?"

"Dr. Webber left for the mainland with the remains."

"You came alone? Didn't I tell you it's not safe?"

"It's not a far walk from the station. Owen and I found something that couldn't wait. It could be exactly what we need to clear your name."

"Great, but if you're killed in the process, my name means nothing."

"I'm fine, Wesley. No harm done. May I come in?"

The idea of her seeing his home caused an uneasiness to whirl deep inside him. He peered over his shoulder at the orange shag rug and living room/dining room that wasn't really a dining room and shifted his feet nervously. "Um...why don't we go see if Tildy has any of her chicken schnitzel left over from dinner?"

"I'm too excited to eat. I want to show you what we found first. I know I'm not an investigator, but this looks really suspicious. Owen searched the Carmichaels' bank statements and found a purchase for a life insurance policy taken out on Jenny four days after she supposedly left you, but before she supposedly died in Malta. How would Calvin Carmichael know to do that unless he knew she was dead?"

Wesley crossed his arms at his chest, studying her enlivened face. The whole thing felt off. "So now you're a forensic accountant? Why are you doing this, Doc? Why are you going above and beyond your duties?"

Her bright-eyed excitement dulled in the porch light. "Because I want to help you."

"Me? Or yourself?" At her squinting eyes

he asked, "Does this have anything to do with that promotion you're after?"

She hesitated a beat, then said, "I told you the promotion was nothing. I've let it go. I knew when I went against Webber's instructions the first day here, my chances of getting it would be gone."

Now Wesley squinted in confusion. "And you stayed anyway? You gave it up just like that. For what?"

"For the truth. And for the safety of the people of Stepping Stones. And for you, whether you want to believe that or not. But I also knew it was what God wanted me to do. He led me here to help. Now, let me in so I can." She lifted her laptop. "It won't take long, and then we can grab a bite if you're that hungry." Lydia stepped up on the threshold as though she meant to bypass him inside, but Wesley leaned into the doorframe to block her.

At her denied passage, abrupt surprise swathed her face. It changed to skepticism real fast.

Always the brilliant thinker.

"Wesley? Why do I get the feeling you don't want me here?" Her pointy chin tilted as her eyes squinted with confusion and hurt.

He hated hurting her, but he kept envisioning her father's elaborate dining room. He couldn't let her in.

"Lydia, look, don't take it personal, okay? I'm the elected sheriff of a small island of everyday folks who can't pay much. My home's not exactly what you're used to."

Her eyes, so close to his, widened again in surprise. "Your home is adorable. What are you talking about? Most people would love to have a cute cottage like yours."

"Your nose is growing, Doc."

Annoyance flashed in her coffee-colored eyes. "So you're back to calling me a liar again? I thought we were past that. Even joking, I don't like it." Her lips puckered, but instead of their desired effect of expressing disappointment in him, they had Wesley's mind sprouting to other ideas. Especially with her close proximity.

Ideas of sweet kisses came to mind. Soft lips beneath his. Tender touches with her long delicate doctor's hands that just might take away what troubled him.

"Well? Are you going to let me by, or not?" she asked.

He dropped his head closer to her lips. The pull to find out overpowered him. "There's a toll," he muttered, barely able to speak over the blood coursing through his head and urging him to take her in his arms.

Lydia inhaled slightly. "What kind of toll?" she asked warily, searching his face and stopping on his lips.

The words *kiss me* sat on his tongue. Would she pull away if he said them? He should tell her to run away.

His throat swelled, and he couldn't speak at all, but his mind had plenty to say. *She's so far out of your league, Grant. In more ways than finances. She's everything good. Hadn't she just proven that when she admitted to giving up the promotion for his island? For her God? You should be protecting her goodness. Protecting her, even from yourself. Especially from yourself.*

Wesley cleared his throat and lifted his

head away. It killed him to, but it was necessary. "Forget it." He pulled the door shut behind him and pushed her back. "I'm hungry. Let's eat."

Pain and surprise eclipsed her face as she clutched her laptop closer to her chest. She frowned at first, then recovered swiftly as she lifted her face to meet his eyes. "Too bad for you, Wesley." She leaned close and whispered, "I would have paid the toll." She pivoted on her heel and took the stairs ahead of him. Her long strides put distance between them while her words confounded him.

"What does that mean?" he called as she stomped up the walkway.

"It means exactly what it sounds like." She swung around. Her shoes crunched on the crushed seashells while she stepped up to him, inches from his face. Her finger jabbed into his chest. "It means I wanted to kiss you, too." Her words should have sounded sweet but instead came out with a sharp edge of bitterness.

"You did?"

"I do." Her hard, glittering eyes turned russet under the lantern streetlights. Her rigid lips pressed hard. They didn't look as though they wanted his touch, contrary to her declaration.

He dropped his gaze to where she clutched her laptop to her chest. "Except I see your barrier is still in place. You keep asking me to trust you, but since the moment we've met, you've lugged your wall around with you. Your tool kit, your laptop, whatever you can put in front of you. What are you afraid of, Doc?"

"I'm not afraid. You don't understand." She looked down at her laptop and relaxed her pinched lips. "I just...I feel like I have to carry this as more of a reminder to myself that I'm qualified."

Shock swamped him. The Doc was insecure about her intelligence? Seriously?

Wesley lifted her chin with his finger and met her eye to eye. "Doc, you're a brilliant woman. Stand tall and lead with that."

She locked her widening pupils on him. Slowly, she brought the computer down to her side and relinquished it to him. He cupped her soft, slender chin. She covered his hand with her own. "Thank you, Wesley" she whispered. "Now I really want to kiss you."

He looked at her waiting lips and smiled back. He had to be crazy for doing this. There were so many reasons to walk away, but at the moment he didn't care about any of them.

Wesley leaned in to meet her lips, selfishly drinking in what Lydia offered him. The sea breeze picked up and stirred around them. So sweet she tasted. Sweet and good.

He wished she could change him for the better. He tilted his head to reach more of her, hoping maybe she could. She felt so right in his arms. Like no other woman ever had. Like she was made for him.

But yet, he knew this couldn't continue.

Wesley pulled away, recognizing that more anger than ever simmered deep down inside him. Anger from knowing she would never be his. She couldn't heal him because he was a lost cause. He would always be poison to her.

The only one who would be changed would

be her. And Wesley didn't need his mother's Proverbs to know it wouldn't be for the better.

Tildy's bouffant, teased beehive high, bobbed with each of her quick steps to Lydia's and Wesley's table. Platters filled with her schnitzel and what looked like everything else from the kitchen graced their plates. Then the flouncy woman disappeared lickety-split. With the heavy atmosphere hanging over their table, Lydia wasn't at all surprised the hostess didn't dally.

Wesley hadn't said a word since they'd kissed. His jaw locked up tighter than she'd ever seen it. Was kissing her really that stressful? She placed her fork by her plate to fold her hands under her chin. "Did you know a human skull contains several bones forming multiple joints on both sides?"

No response. Nothing but a fork twirl in his sauerkraut.

She touched the sides of her jaw to demonstrate. "The temporomandibular joint joins the lower jawbone called the mandible to the temporal bone in the skull. The joint facilitates the movements of our lower jaw in activities like talking and eating." She eyed his food that he'd yet to eat, even though he supposedly had been so hungry. "Any misalignment of the bones while biting can bring about increased tension in the joint, resulting in lockjaw. It causes severe pain and inability to move the lower jaw."

He dropped his fork. The clatter brought up a few heads from the patrons around them. "What's your point?" he asked.

"Ah, so you can talk. I just wanted to make sure I didn't need to rush you over to the clinic for a bad case of tetanus."

He flapped his jaw, demonstrating it was in working order. "I'm fine. I just lost my appetite."

So kissing had been a bad experience for him.

She hoped her face stayed straight and gave nothing away. She averted her attention to the enormous amount of food on their plates. "Does Tildy feed you like this every night? The portions are huge."

"Close, but no. I think Tildy went a little overboard tonight because I'm with you."

"Me? Why me?"

The tic was back. The urge to reach out and rub his temporomandibular joints had to be restrained. Thankfully, he released it on his own before her fingers went to town. "I don't usually bring ladies here with me, unless…" He paused. "Well, unless things are pretty serious. It's kind of like bringing them home to meet the parents. Don't pay Tildy any attention. She doesn't know this is a business dinner."

The idea of this dinner being business only made Lydia feel as if she were being passed over on the Wall of Flowers again. Passed over for all the dainty, petite ladies of Wesley's past. The ones he escorted here on his arm for more than business.

She cleared her throat. "What happened outside between us didn't feel like business to me. Can we talk about it?"

His ice-blue eyes flashed cold. "There's no point. We need to keep things business only. It… We can't be anything more."

"Because you don't go for tall, lanky, four-eyed women with the freakish ability to recite *the periodic table* while formulating chemical components of DNA?"

"Women like that are smart enough to stay as far away from me as possible."

A shadow fell over their already dark table. Lydia lifted her gaze to find Derek looming over them.

"Well, isn't this sweet?" His hands reached for the edge of the table. "While Patty sits in a jail cell for a crime she didn't commit, you two are out on a date?" Derek leaned close to Lydia's face. "I thought I warned you, Dr. Muir. You better be careful who you dine with. Things aren't always as they seem."

Wesley's chair scraped along the wooden floor as he pushed to stand.

"Derek!" Tildy reemerged from wherever she'd been hiding. She nipped the brawl between the men in the bud like a professional barmaid. A few shakes of her towel was all it took. "You leave them alone, or you won't be welcome here anymore," she scolded Derek and herded him to a place at the bar, but his lethal stare continued to zing Lydia from across the room.

She veered around to sever the hold it had on her. "To think I actually liked that man when I first met him." Her hand went to her throat to take in a deep breath, but something hard beneath her blouse met her fingers.

The ruby.

"You're still wearing that thing?" Wesley asked with displeasure.

"I told you it's the safest—"

"I know what you told me, but you also know how much it bothers me to see it on you. It could get you killed. But then, maybe it's more important for you to constantly remind me of our status differences. Don't worry, Doc. I already know."

His flippant accusation shocked her into silence. Sure, he probably thought he was sparring with her again, but this time she had to wonder if these really were jokes or the truth of how he really saw her.

Lydia's fingers trembled as she reached for her laptop. As she stood, she brought the laptop to her chest, then immediately dropped it down to her side. "Why do you continue to insinuate I'm insincere? You make me feel like a specimen under a microscope. Like I have to prove myself to you constantly. I know I'm not beautiful, and I may not be the life of the party, but I do my best to be trustworthy and honest in everything I do. I don't deserve your unfounded judgments thrown in my face, especially when I've given you the benefit of the doubt and believed in you when many of your own townspeople haven't. I've put my life in your hands numerous times. I've done my best to help you in every way possible. I gave up a promotion for you."

Lydia felt a surge of anger in her, but she reined it in. What she had to say would be said with a level head. "But no matter what I do, you still don't trust me. And the truth is, you never will. But that's your problem. Not mine."

Lydia breathed deep and caught the other customers gawking. She wouldn't let them deter her from doing what she knew she had to do. "The fact that you would think for even a nanosecond that I am so shallow to believe

I'm better than you because of a bank account shows me you don't know me at all and you have no desire to get to know me. You've already made up your mind about me, and nothing I do or say will change that. So you can keep on walking by, Wesley Grant. This wallflower doesn't pick you." Her voice trembled a bit. She steadied it before saying, "Goodbye, *Sheriff.* I'll be leaving in the morning for good."

Lydia swept by the staring patrons and out the front entrance. She raced as fast as she could along the boardwalk and up Main Street. Her side cramped, slowing her to a walk, but the pain in her chest stopped her completely.

Her palm rushed at her cheeks to catch the falling tears with her free hand. She removed her glasses to clear her vision, scolding herself for loving a man who would treat her so coldly without reason.

Loving him?

Yes, she loved him, all right. She probably fell in love with him when she fell for all his lies about his innocence. If he could be so cold to her, then why couldn't he kill in cold blood? Maybe Derek was right. Maybe things weren't as they seemed. Maybe she'd been protecting the killer this whole time.

Well, no more.

Lydia gave a last swipe across her eyes and set off in the direction of the sheriff's station. Two steps in and she was yanked back, her mouth and nose sealed over by a hand wrapped in leather.

Lydia's laptop and glasses fell to her feet, forgotten. Her hands dug at the gloved hand while her lungs screamed for air. With her mouth and nose covered, no life-giving oxygen could pass through. Her thoughts jumbled into a tangled mess as she fought for her life alone on this dark street.

Then the unmistakable impact of a gun jammed into her back and one thought became clear as day. She'd better start leaving trace evidence behind.

Or she would never be found.

"What are you all looking at?" Wesley spouted off at the islanders still gawking at him even after ten minutes. "Haven't you ever seen a guy get dumped before?"

"Wesley." Tildy dragged a chair out and sat. "Don't be mad at them. We all care about you. And your gal, too."

"She's not my gal. You heard her. She's leaving." And his chest had never ached so badly in his life. How was he still breathing?

"Leaving because you pushed her away." Tildy leaned in. "Are you listening to me?"

Listening? He could barely hear her over the sound of Lydia's farewell blaring in his head. "You're no better than your mother." Tildy's words pulled him back with a jolt.

"What are you talking about, Tildy?" he demanded. "What about my mother?"

"Do you want to know why you're pushing that wonderful girl out of your life when all you really want to do is hold on to her and never let her go? Well, I'll tell you why. It's for the same reason your mother pushed you out."

Wesley stilled. Would he finally know the answer to the question that plagued him?

Tildy sat back and sighed. "Don't get me

wrong. Sarah was my best friend. I loved her dearly, and I've tried to fill in for her since her death, because that's what she asked of me. But I never agreed with what she did to you."

"Did to me? You mean like why she told me to go back to school because she was out of the woods of danger. That her cancer was gone? That she lied?"

Tildy nodded solemnly. "She pushed you out to protect you from the pain of watching her die. She loved you so much, but she didn't think you could handle it."

"Then she didn't trust me."

"And how does it feel not to be trusted? Because you're doing the same thing to that girl." Tildy pointed to the obscure darkness through the glass door. "You've pushed her out because you don't think she can handle the pain that is in you."

"You don't get it. I don't want her to ever change because of me."

"Just like the favor your mother did for you. If she had told you she had two months left, what would you have done?"

"I would have stayed. I would have helped her. I would have made her time left the best it could be."

"All admirable things." Tildy smiled and covered his hand with hers. "They're also the same things your gal wants to do for you. But without your confidence in her, she can't. Her hands are tied. By you. And I hate to tell you this, but by not trusting her, you're changing her anyway. A gal who doesn't have her man's trust feels squashed down. Broken. A gal who does have her man's trust will bring him—"

"Stop," Wesley said. "I know this one. Her husband trusts her, and she will bring him good, and never harm, all the days of his life. Mom drilled it into me. Always said the husband had a part to fill, too."

"She was a good, smart woman. Don't fault her for thinking she was doing you a favor in her final days."

Tears filled Wesley's eyes. He squeezed his thumb and finger into his eyes to press them back. He sniffed and laughed a little nervously. "I always knew I was more like her than Dad."

Tildy pushed his phone across the table toward him. "Call Lydia and fix this tonight. Tomorrow could be too late. In fact, it might already be too late. Derek's probably giving her a ride back right now."

"Derek?" Wesley shot a look to the empty stool where his ex-deputy had been sitting. "Where is he? When did he leave?" Wesley jumped to his feet and raced to the door.

"He left right after Lydia did. Why? What's the problem?"

Wesley pushed through the doors without answering her and speed-dialed the station as he raced up to the street. "Owen, it's me," he said into the phone when his deputy picked up. "Let me talk to Lydia."

"Lydia's not here. I thought she was with you."

"She left about half an hour ago. She's not back yet?" Wesley scanned the darkness up and down the empty street. He could see the lights from the station from here. It shouldn't have taken her this long to get back there.

I shouldn't have let her go alone. I knew it wasn't safe. Not after all her brushes with death. Not with that thing around her neck.

And now she could be in danger again.

He grabbed at his hair where panic seized his head. "Owen, put out a search for her. And for Derek, too. I'm going down to the shore in case she went for a walk."

"That's probably what she did, man. Don't worry, we'll find her."

"We need to do more than find her, Owen. We need to find her alive."

FOURTEEN

Lydia pried at the large, gloved hand covering her nose and mouth. A man's strength yanked her back into the probe of the gun. If asphyxiation wasn't her cause of death, a gunshot wound would be.

Sharp-needled pain seized her lungs. Her fingers clawed at the leather pressed so tight over her airways, but it was no use. She lacked a muscular system to fight off her attacker.

"Move," the man whispered harshly into her ear, his cheek pricked hers with sharp bristles. The abrasion no match for the slicing ache in her chest.

She needed air.

She whimpered and stumbled forward under his forceful direction. He didn't let up his grip.

Stars of light flashed overhead that had

nothing to do with the cosmos above. Time was running out to save herself. *Think!* The thought that her bony elbows might make for a sharp rib jab was shattered when the sharper piece of metal in her back found the intercostal space between her ribs and dug its point in loud and clear.

She wasn't in any position to fight off anyone, especially in her air-deprived state. Her feet tripped, nearly sending her flying. Proof that she could barely stand up, never mind take control of the situation.

Her feet tripped again, causing the man to move his finger just enough for air to fill one of her nostrils. She dragged hard to pull as much oxygen in as possible. With her lungs refilling, Lydia could focus enough to realize she'd been led down to the shore.

She felt the squishy, sinking sand beneath her shoes. It was the sand that tripped her up before. A scan of her surroundings said they were headed to the large boathouse outlined in the distance and jutting out on the water. Was he taking her on a boat? She couldn't let him take her off dry land. There would be no way to leave a trail.

Lydia whined again, shaking her head to try to loosen his grasp.

"You knew this was coming. I told you that you'd be next."

Derek! The voice sounded like Derek's, and so did the warning. Except had his warning really been a promise?

They approached the red building, its door ajar and its glass window revealing pitch-black darkness inside. At least out here, the moon's glow outlined her surroundings. In there, she might as well be blindfolded.

Lydia twisted at the threshold, but Derek shoved her to the hard, wooden floor. Pain struck where she landed on her right arm as the door slammed behind her. She screamed out.

"Don't bother. No one can hear you."

Her chest heaved. "Why are you doing this?" She flipped her body over and leaned back on her hands. Rough floorboards stretched beneath her.

"Because one way or another, Wesley is going down for murder. If not Jenny's, then yours."

"You're going to kill me so Wesley goes to jail? Why?"

"Because that's where he belongs!" Derek's voice reached high into the rafters. "He should have been arrested five years ago, but Patty just had to help him. Why couldn't she ever see he didn't care about her? I won't let him pin this on her. I have to protect her. And once you're dead, everyone will have to face the fact that he's a killer. And Patty won't be able to help him this time."

"But he's not a killer," she said to the dark outline that was Derek. He hovered over her, his round shape a dead giveaway, but not as deadly as the gun she knew he held on her. "Please, Derek, don't do this. It won't fix anything."

"If he's put in jail, it will fix everything. You already gave him motive to kill you with your farewell speech back there. Lots of witnesses saw it, too."

The gun cocked with a jolting click. Lydia

turned her face to the left. If only Wesley knew she needed help. If only she hadn't told him goodbye. Then maybe he would come looking for her. *God, I need Your help.* Her lips moved in a silent outcry. She trusted her Lord to come to her rescue, but she also knew she had to do her part. But what could she do? With the extreme darkness in the building, she could barely see in front of her face. *Lord, make my paths straight and keep my efforts on target.*

Lydia rolled onto her right side with her long legs sweeping out in front of her. Fear of throwing herself blindly into nothingness had to be put aside for the impact her shins made.

Bull's-eye.

Derek let out a grunt and, in the next second, landed down on her with his full, heavy weight. Air whooshed out from her lungs as her arms flailed to be free of him. Her fingers met the pudgy flesh of his face and dug deep. If she could get DNA under her nails, the M.E. would know Wesley didn't kill her. She might die tonight, but she would do whatever she could to exonerate Wesley—even if somewhere deep inside her she wondered if he would do the same for her.

Derek ripped her hands from his face in a beseeching cry. "Stop! Please stop! I'm not going to hurt you, okay? I thought I could, but I can't. I just can't."

Lydia stilled her hands, realizing Derek had her wrists in a tight grasp. But that also meant the gun was gone. He must have dropped it when she'd swept his legs out from under him.

Was this the reason for his change in plans? Or was he realizing he wasn't a killer after all? Lydia hoped for the latter but didn't take the chance to find out.

She could barely get a breath in with his weight pressing into her lungs, but she managed to fling out her arms to break free of his grasp and shove at his chest. A roll back to her left and she broke free completely. She scampered away across the planks with quick agility. Her hands felt for safety until her path ended with a collision into the hard hull of a stored boat.

Lord, this can't be the end.

"Lydia, I'm sorry," Derek said, the distance of his voice telling her he hadn't moved closer to her, but he was standing again. Remorse also came through his pleading voice. Maybe she could believe she was safe now. She leaned back against the boat, debating whether to relax her flight mode or not. "I was wrong. I—"

The floorboards vibrated beneath her as something hard hit them with impact.

"Derek?" Lydia peered into the darkness and still saw the outline of Derek, so it couldn't have been him who fell. She could see his tall legs step closer to her, but the image didn't compute. Derek didn't have tall legs like these. He was round, not lean. This wasn't Derek standing before her anymore.

Wesley?

Lydia's heart jumped to her throat. Wesley had come to help her after all. She scurried to her feet to jump into his arms. Safety beckoned an arm's length away. But before she could fall into those strong, comforting arms, searing pain cut into the back of her neck.

The necklace. Wesley wanted the necklace? After he said he detested it?

Had it been him who tried for it at the museum? Had it been him who nearly choked the life out of her for a stone?

Lydia couldn't focus enough to figure it out. Tears sprang from her eyes and flowed down her cheeks. The clasp held fast at her neck. She wished it would break. Lydia grabbed on to the hand fisting the ruby at her throat. "Please," she squeaked out through the cutting agony.

"Beg all you want," her attacker whispered. "This time I'm not leaving until I get what I came for, even if I have to remove your head to get it."

This isn't Wesley. Lydia didn't know who had her life in their hands.

"I was hoping Deputy Boy would do you in. Then I could cut the rock off you and be long gone before anyone found your body. Too bad he chickened out. But I won't. I can't. Too much is at stake, and you know too much." He yanked tighter, pulling her face so close, she could feel the heat of his breath.

The voice plagued her memory. She knew she heard it before, even with the man whispering. But where?

Lydia couldn't wait to find out. She brought quick, eye-jabbing fingers up in the same moment as her very sharp knee.

The man fell to his knees, crying out. His voice clicked in her mind, but all she could focus on was escaping into the dark. *Stay with me, God,* she pleaded. *I need Your guidance more than ever.*

"Please tell me she's at the station," Wesley answered on the first ring of his cell.

"Afraid not." Owen sighed. "But, Wes, we found her glasses and laptop in the street. This doesn't look good."

No, he wouldn't let his mind go there. "It's a small island. She can't be far."

"A small island with a lot of water around it. Miriam can attest to that. You know how up close and personal she came with it, or rather under it, last year when someone tried to drown her."

Nausea rolled in the pit of Wesley's stomach as he stared at the ocean spreading out before him like spilling ink. He'd never find her if someone hid her in its deep dark depths. At least not until she washed ashore. *If* she washed ashore.

But after the helicopter crash, Lydia proved she could hold her own in the ocean. In fact, she held him up, as well. He couldn't let her down now.

"Start a search party. Get every man and woman available. I want every barn and doghouse searched, twice. I'm going out on my boat."

Wesley clipped his phone to his waist and trudged through thick sand to reach his private boat docked behind his cabin. His knees hit the landing at full force while his hands cranked to release the rope from its metal cleat. He was in the boat before the rope was freed, left to unwind and flap behind in the water as the boat set out in the direction of town. The mounted side searchlight illuminated the water directly in front of him, but it was a small consolation for sunlight.

Houselights lit the coastline; more flicked

on as he passed. People were coming out to help find Lydia. Gratitude helped him breathe easier. The islanders would put together a top-notch search and rescue. He hoped he wouldn't need it.

"Lydia, where are you? Please be hiding out because of what I said. Not because someone has you."

The wooden pier attached to the boardwalk jutted out into the sea off in the distance. The last place he'd seen her. The place she'd walked out on. He knew his words had been hurtful even before he'd said them, and still, he'd said them.

Wesley passed the boathouse. Its glass windows reflected the moonlight back at him. His floodlight also bounced back at him off the glass. He zipped past and approached the pier. High above him the lanterns were lit along the railings, but not a shadow of a person stood out. He turned the boat around to take another sweep of the coastline. A flash from the boathouse's windows caught his attention.

He was too far away for it to be his spot-light—and the moon didn't flash.

Someone was inside with a flashlight.

Wesley adjusted the throttle to pick up speed. He grabbed the phone at his waist and called Owen on speed dial. Voice mail picked up. "Someone's in the boathouse. That's where you'll find me," he said and brought his boat in.

The boat dock void of vessels gave him ample space to pull up. He cut the engine and drifted in on silence, except for the soft swish of water that the bow of his boat cut. His portside hull hit the wood of the dock and bounced once, then twice with a dull thud. Wesley grabbed his rope and gave a couple twists to the waiting cleat before he hopped up in stealthy silence. His shoes barely cracked the wooden planks as he skulked down the berth.

The entrance door was shut but unlocked. He left the door open when he stepped inside, his back pressed to the right side wall while he strained to hear any sounds in the dark-ness. Nothing at first caught his attention.

Until footsteps raced across the second-floor balcony. A screech filled the rafters followed by "Let me go!"

Lydia!

Wesley ran to the steps he knew were against the right wall. He didn't need lights but worked from memory, having been in this boathouse a million times since birth. He took the steps two at a time, but before he reached the landing, he heard Lydia grunt as though someone hit her. He had to make his move before she was hurt more. Wesley followed the scuffling sounds to the balcony and made out an outline of two people struggling against a single wooden railing.

The broader of the two people was his main focus as he rammed into the fray. A quick punch to the gut doubled the man over, but in the next moment, the big guy retaliated by taking Wesley's air right from his lungs with a head butt to his midsection. Wesley careened back into the railing at full force. Cracking wood caused him to roll to his right and away from the compromised railing—and out of the path of another assault.

His attacker came out of the darkness again, but this time he plowed right into the railing. The wood broke with a deafening snap, but nothing compared to the shout of terror ringing through the old building as the man careened off the balcony to the first floor.

"Lydia!" Wesley called out, searching the darkness for her. "Where are you?"

A body came at him, wrapping frenzied but beautiful bony arms around him. He rejoiced in finding her alive. "Are you hurt?" he said into her hair. At the shake of her head, he asked, "Who's the guy? Is it Derek?"

She shook her head again. A hiccup in her breaths stopped her from answering right away. "It's Carmichael," she whispered finally.

"Calvin Carmichael?" Wesley didn't have time to figure the whys out. He had to get her to safety and Carmichael in custody. "Get to the third floor. There's an exit that leads to an outside stairwell. Take it and get to the street."

"What about you?" Her voice hitched.

"Don't worry about me, just do as I say."

"I can't leave you here." Her forehead dropped to his, her breaths fast and short.

"You can and you will." He wished he could see her face, but he reached a hand to cup her cheek to at least feel her beauty. "Lydia, I need to know that you're safe before I go down there." He pressed his cheek to hers and whispered into her ear, "Now go."

She crawled to the stairs. He heard her ascend as he'd asked, then he stood and made his way down to the first floor. He took the steps sideways with his back to the wall, unsure of what he would find, or what would find him.

Would Carmichael be injured or dead from the fall? Or was his late fiancée's father waiting for his chance to finally do him in?

The fact that it was Carmichael whom he hunted confounded Wesley. Had the man killed his own daughter? Wesley bit his tongue from calling out and asking. As much as he wanted to know, he couldn't risk giving up his location.

A heavy engine rumbled loudly. Carmichael turned something on, which meant he survived the fall. Wesley placed the sound as a piece of machinery that could only be the forklift used to lift the smaller boats from the water.

What could the man possibly want with a forklift?

Wesley stepped down off the bottom stair. Headlights on the machine turned on and blinded him, but before he could raise an arm as a shield, the engine chugged loud and headed toward him.

A swift dive back up the stairs saved him from the prongs of the lift. They struck the wooden walls of the boathouse right where he'd been standing. The stairs vibrated beneath him as he realized what Calvin planned to do with the forklift.

Impale him.

The machine beeped with its reversal warnings. The hydraulic lifts screamed as they were raised to a height that would find their target—unless Wesley could hijack the forklift.

Wesley jumped to his feet and prepared for the machinery to return. The beeping stopped and the forklift plowed forward again just as Wesley expected. He stood ready, hands out, a bounce to his step. As the steel lifts jutted at him, he jumped up on one. From his perch, Wesley made a dive for the front window opening while his fist made contact with Calvin's face.

Earsplitting beeps resounded. Somehow they'd shifted into Reverse at full speed. Wesley reached for the controls, but Carmichael took aim with a chin jab that sent Wesley flying back. Through the stars, it took all his strength to hold on to the metal framework of the machine as his legs swung out beneath him.

Something collided with the moving lift bringing it to a jarring halt. All at once, Wesley's teeth jammed up on the impact, his hold on the window frame came loose and his body flew back into the open window.

He collided into Calvin. The engine screamed.

Wesley took a head butt from Calvin and a shoulder shove that allowed his opponent to jump from the driver's seat. Wesley dived out and attacked from behind, sending them both sprawling to the floor.

They rolled one way, then another before colliding with the hull of a boat. Wesley reached for the man's arm and twisted it up behind his back. He yanked him to his feet just as something tiny but hard pinged off his head. The sharp pain had him grabbing at his hairline when another small object hit his back, followed by a few more.

Nails, he realized. Nails were popping out of the ceiling. Wesley stared up in confusion, then down the silhouette of the main support pole in the middle of the boathouse.

The very pole the forklift had hit and was still pushing on at full force.

The building was about to collapse!

Wesley made a grab for Carmichael's shoulder to haul him out of there before it was too late. But in the next second, pain exploded at the front of his neck. Carmichael had swung around and heaved the edge of his hand right into Wesley's jugular so hard and quick that all Wesley could do was crumple to the floor like a marionette with its strings cut. Flat on his back, he grabbed at his neck for air. His windpipe felt crushed, and air barely threaded through. Never had he been so immobilized by the strike of someone's hand. Bright splotches of light burst in front of his eyes.

Carmichael leaned over him. "All Jennifer had to do was give it back," he said, and then ran out of the building as more nails rained down.

Wesley needed to get out of there, too, but his body failed to move. More nails rained down on him with sharp stings that he barely noticed over the swelling and closing of his throat and the aching of his lungs.

The whole building let out a horrid groan.

All he could do was lay there and wheeze while the walls wobbled like a Jell-O mold. He could see the boards from the rafters snapping like twigs. He could feel bits of debris raining down around him.

Then the shadow of a person loomed over him.

"Wesley, you need to move!"

Lydia! What was she doing here?

"Come on, Wesley! This building's coming down!"

His arms were pulled up behind him; the pain in his sockets clicked his brain into gear. Lydia had come back for him. She was trying to pull him out.

His mouth opened to yell, "No! Leave me! Get out!" But no sound came out of his injured throat.

Wesley had accepted his death, but he could not accept that Lydia would be crushed right beside him.

Lydia could tell by the way he grabbed at his throat and by his short wheezes that his brachial plexus had sustained a blunt-force trauma. She hoped his vagus nerve, which is attached to every major organ in the body, hadn't been struck. But she wouldn't know until she could find shelter to assess the damage.

The closest place was the inside of the boat next to them. If she could get him inside and under the bow, they might survive the collapse of the roof. At least the balconies with all the stored boats weren't above them. Still, the roof wouldn't feel good when it fell on them.

She heaved and tried another pull on his arms, but Wesley yanked her back, his face awash with anger as his lips formed the word *go*.

"I'm not going anywhere without you. Now help me get you into the boat before we're both dead."

Wesley stilled as he studied her. His wheezing stretched out a little longer and she thought he was getting a little more air in now. *Good*. She really didn't want to have to perform an emergency tracheotomy. It would only be a tiny hole to open his airway, but in her line of work, the people she sliced open were already dead. She never had to worry about actually killing someone.

She touched him gently on the chest. His eyes locked on hers. An inner battle waged on in them. Would he push her away? "Wesley, please let me help you."

He lifted an arm, but not to push her away. Instead he wrapped it around her neck so she could assist him to his knees. Lydia sighed in relief at his compliancy. At the stern of the boat, she hefted him up while he used whatever strength he had in him to get himself up and over the side. She followed him in and landed with a thud on her back; her own air expelled in a whoosh.

A falling piece of wood landed on her arm. "Ah!" she yelled out, pulling it free and flipping over in a rush. "Up here. It'll protect us." She pulled him up into the bow just as the building let out its loudest, most sickening moan yet. Debris hit the steel covering over them, each pinging sound jerking her reflexes as she waited for the big one.

The big one that could kill them.

Lydia twisted to face Wesley. She wished she could see his face but felt her way until his rough cheek filled her hand. She focused on his breathing that seemed a little more even now, less wheezing. Had he been saved from one death only to be crushed instead?

"Why?" he croaked out. A good sign that the swelling was receding.

"When I got to the third floor, I couldn't

leave you." Something big and heavy landed on top of the boat and shifted it on its stand. Lydia let out a scream as Wesley tightened his hold on her, cradling her head as they braced for another fall.

Thunder crackled above. *No,* not thunder, but the wood splintering into tiny sharp and heavy fragments. A piece crashed down and tipped the boat onto its side. Lydia screamed again as another hit pelted them, followed by a trembling whoosh.

"Hold on!" Wesley shouted hoarsely, and tucked her face into his chest.

The rest of the structure rushed down at them with the force of an angry stampede. She dug her nails into his arms and shoulders, her eyes scrunched closed and her teeth locked tight while she prayed to God to end it.

Then the boat stilled, and the falling timber stopped. The motor from the forklift sputtered and then ceased, as well.

Neither of them dared move. Her breathing hitched a few times, but surprisingly in this sheer moment of terror, her lungs didn't seize in any kind of panic.

"I'm not scared, Wesley." She gave a little nervous laugh. "Isn't that crazy? I should be hyperventilating right now, knowing that we're probably going to suffocate under here, but God is with us, and He's giving us His peace."

"Peace?" he croaked through the pain. "Is that whose peace I see when I watch you? God's?" He sounded like he had a bad case of laryngitis. She knew every word had to feel like razor blades slicing the inside of his throat. Her heart ached for him.

"Shh." She found his lips with her fingers. "Don't talk."

"Is it?" He took her hand in his.

"Yes, God gives me His peace when I follow His plan for me. It's when I don't feel His peace that I know I'm not following Him."

"But you feel His peace now, and He led you under a collapsed roof. I don't understand."

She sighed. "It may not make sense to us now, but there's a reason, and somehow, He will turn this horrible event for good. Even if we're not here to see it for ourselves. That's

His promise you can trust in. And when you believe it, the peace comes."

His forehead fell to hers while his hand held the back of her neck. "I love...I love how your strength and your faith rise up in the face of trouble. I hope someday I can stand as strong as you."

That would imply they survived the night. Lydia thought it best to keep Wesley thinking positive and said, "With God leading you, you will. Keep Him by your side always."

"What if I want you beside me, too?"

Lydia inhaled a little extra oxygen, then sealed her lips tight as Wesley's question lingered between them. Her eyes drifted closed even though the black shroud of darkness allowed for anonymity.

"I take it you don't feel the same way."

Lydia started and stopped and started again. "I would like nothing more than to be a part of your life here on Stepping Stones."

"But?"

She sighed, her breath warm on his cheek. "Wesley, I have a career that I know God has called me to. He's given me a gift I have to use."

"Use it here with me. I think we make a great team. Your forensics knowledge would be really helpful."

"Stepping Stones isn't actually a hotbed of crime. Besides, I already spend my days proving guilt and innocence for other people. I don't think I could spend my days proving my love to you, too."

"Love? Are you saying you love me?"

Lydia floundered in the hole she dug for herself.

"The truth. I want the truth, Lydia. Do you love me?"

"Love doesn't matter."

"What if I told you I loved you?"

"I would say I don't believe you. Your actions have shown I can't trust you any more than you trust me."

His silence felt stifling. The lack of air made her lightheaded and didn't help. She wondered how much more time they had.

Was this really how things would end for them? Bitter to the end?

"I'm sorry." His whisper was more like a breath, but she heard it loud and clear. "I know I've been horrible to you. Please forgive me. Please."

Lydia scrunched her eyes tight at his plea. She wanted to believe it was more than a dying man's last wish for his own solace, but too much had been said not to make her wary.

And so she let her silence be her answer.

"Wes!" A muffled voice shouted to them from somewhere outside, slicing their heavy sadness. It was Owen. "Are you in here?"

"Help is here. You're going to be okay," Wesley whispered, then croaked out, "Yes!" He barely made a sound and started coughing.

Lydia winced knowing his throat brutally hurt. She rested a tentative hand on his chest. "Let me," she said and shouted back, "We're in here! We're in a boat, but we're all covered!"

"Keep talking, so we can follow you."

Boards could be heard being strewn about as Lydia shouted back and forth with Owen. Finally a break in their covering allowed them to be pulled out to safety and big gulps of fresh air.

The whole town had shown up to help free them. Lanterns hung from poles and from the hands of townspeople. Tears welled up in Lydia's eyes as she thanked and hugged each of them, loving each one like family. She would be forever grateful to them.

"We'll go to the mainland tomorrow to have them arraigned," she heard Owen saying to Wesley.

"Them?" she asked Wesley when Owen left his side.

Wesley removed the ice pack from his throat to speak. He still had to whisper, but the swelling subsided. "Owen apprehended Calvin Carmichael making a mad dash for his boat. He also found Derek in the debris. Derek's at the clinic now, but he'll be going to Rockland tomorrow to be arraigned, too. He admitted to trying to kill you. Why didn't you tell me?"

She shrugged. "He wouldn't have followed through. He was just angry about Patty being in jail."

"Not true. He may not have been after the ruby, but he did cut the helicopter's fuel line. He hated me so much he didn't think about your safety at all."

Lydia frowned. "The truth can be really ugly when you uncover it."

"Sometimes, but we both have jobs that require us to do it regardless."

"Right, and I need to get back to mine before I lose it completely. I'll be ready to go with you in the morning."

She expected his jaw to tick with displeasure. She expected to hear one of his typical snide comments.

Except when a passing lantern cast a glimmer of light over Wesley's face, she saw no clenched jaw. She saw only sadness and remorse. And when he opened his mouth the only comment that came out was "As you wish." Then he turned to help his islanders with securing the area, leaving her alone with the ugly truth.

He'd asked for forgiveness, and she withheld it.

FIFTEEN

Calvin Carmichael turned green right before Wesley's eyes. The two-hour boat ride to the mainland must not have sat well with his prisoner. Of course, the gun Wesley held on him the whole way probably didn't help.

"How does it feel to be the one in cuffs, Carmichael?" Wesley rasped out, his throat still burning from the man's hit. "I can't say I'm surprised to find out you're not so squeaky clean."

Calvin sat about four feet from Derek, both men handcuffed to their metal armrests. But Calvin did nothing but stare out to sea.

He seemed to have checked out of mind and body. Not one threat or even tactful play on his emotions caused a stir in his composure. It was as though he was inhuman.

But then, he *was* a coldhearted killer, one

who'd murdered his only daughter. And who knew how many people dug their own graves mining for rocks so he could line his pockets?

"Did Jenny steal the ruby for you? Or *before* you? That is what you planned. Smuggle it in through the museum, then stage a theft. At my expense, mind you, but we'll get to that later. Something must have happened to put Jenny in danger. Did she steal it for you and not give it back? Is that why she had to die? Must have made you pretty mad when she swallowed it right in front of you. How dare she? That was *your* deal you worked so hard for, right?"

Nothing. No response but a head turned away.

"Don't you get it?" Wesley asked, almost losing his patience. "Your life is over."

Carmichael turned back and opened his mouth for the first time since last night. "Finally, Sheriff Grant, you're right about something."

Owen interrupted from the wheel, "Wes, we're here. There's a uniform ready to assist us to the courthouse." The engine cut, and the boat drifted to the dock. Owen twisted his head to his side and spoke over his shoulder. "Lydia, you sure you're okay to walk?"

She hadn't said a word during the trip, but Wesley had felt her presence the whole way. He felt her intelligent brown eyes bore into his back while he stood guard. It took all his strength not to turn his head to her, knowing this would be the last time he would ever see her again. She'd made her choice, and it wasn't him. Not that he blamed her. He got everything he deserved.

She stood from her seat, dressed exactly as she had the first day he met her. The day she stepped off the boat and onto his island. She wore the same professional suit and carried the same tool kit, clutched in front of her—not out of fear, though. He knew now she held it there because it was her way of showing the world she was qualified for the job. "Yes, I can walk," she answered Owen's question, then looked at Wesley. "But before I leave, may I ask Mr. Carmichael a question?"

Wesley nodded. "Go ahead."

"Mr. Carmichael," she spoke to the man. "Why did you blow up your boat?"

"I didn't. It was stolen."

"Stolen? Or bartered?" she asked quickly.

Calvin's eyes locked on hers without a response.

"I only ask because I noticed a few things in your home missing. The foyer table. The large painting on the wall at the top of the stairs. For them to be showcased at your home's entrance they had to be pretty valuable. Like your yacht."

Wesley smiled at this woman, loving the way her mind worked. He was going to miss working with her. If only he had done things right, she could have been his partner for life. "Interesting assessment, Dr. Muir. I think I see where you're going with this. Mr. Carmichael was indebted to someone." Wesley turned to the man. "Is she right? You have someone to pay off? Is that what this ruby was supposed to do? And when Jennifer swallowed it, you tried to get it back. Albeit, a little gruesomely. That's got to be one hefty bill you owe for you to do such a thing, wouldn't you agree, Doc?"

Wesley turned back to Lydia to find her disembarking. His stomach clenched. Their time of teaming up had come to an end. This was the last time he would see his love.

His love. Yes, she was definitely his love. And she would remain a part of him always. In his heart and in his mind, he would forever remember this brilliant and noble woman standing before him. A woman worth far more than the ruby at her neck, worth more than all the rubies in the world.

But most importantly, he would remember how his distrust in her pushed her away.

He had to be honest with himself if he wanted to make a positive change in his life. But more important, he had to be honest with God because it was Him who would be doing the changing. *And thank You, Lord, for that. I'm going to need all the help I can get. But my first step is to face the truth of my sins.*

The truth was he allowed his past experiences with Jenny, his framing in Boston and even his mom's choices to lead him in his daily life. Those things may not have been his sins, but his actions because of them were. And now, he had to accept the consequences of a life without his love.

Owen stepped up to her side, offering her his arm. A twinge of jealousy stirred in Wesley. It would be Owen who got to hold her hand one last time before she left. Not him. "It was wonderful to meet you," Owen said, helping her up on the dock.

Lydia nodded and looked back at Wesley. "Goodbye, Wesley."

He nodded, unable to say goodbye because his throat closed tighter than it had last night. He put his attention back on his captives, but strained to hear her footsteps as she retreated down the long wooden dock. Each clomp of her heels resounded over the waves and the rushing blood pounding in his head until the last of her footfalls ushered her out of his life forever.

"I see it's back to work for this anthropologist," Lydia announced to Dr. Webber as soon as she entered her lab. She'd come right

from the harbor to find he stood over a partially decomposed male cadaver on her lab
table. "People don't stop dying, Miss Muir,
just because you take a vacation," he replied
as he removed facial tissue to expose the
skull structure. Parts of bone were missing
on half of the victim's face and would need
to be recreated before he could be identified.

"GSW to the face?" she asked as she opened
her metal locker to grab her lab coat. A reflection of herself in her locker mirror showed
the ruby at her neck. She quickly unclasped
it. A scan of her lab behind her showed the
box with all her evidence from the island on
the counter. Once the ruby was locked back
up in its rightful place, Lydia breathed a sigh
of relief. It felt good to get that horrid thing
off her, once and for all.

"Gunshot wound to the face would be the
correct assessment," Dr. Webber confirmed.
"A restaurant owner found him in her Dump-
ster this morning. The police suspect it to be
gang related. But the only job we have is to
find out who he is…or was."

"I can take it from here." She snapped on her latex gloves and stepped up to the table.

"Are you sure? You just returned." He peered over his glasses. "Don't you want to get a cup of coffee or something?"

Lydia smirked in surprise. "Why, Dr. Webber, that's the nicest thing you've ever said to me."

"Yeah, about that." He straightened to his full height and met her eye-to-eye. "I'm sorry about how I treated you these last few years. I've been doing a lot of thinking about what your gentleman said. You are a good forensic anthropologist. Great even. I should have given you the respect you deserved. Not make you pay for my bruised ego from an issue I had with your father years ago. You have a good man in that sheriff."

Lydia smiled. "He is good, but he's not mine."

"Really?" The old man's face of wrinkles pinched up like a prune. But something else caught her attention. Underneath his confused look, Lydia realized the antagonism she usually witnessed in him was gone. "I know I'm old, but I could have sworn the love bug had bitten the two of you."

Lydia grinned at the expression but stopped when her boss continued saying, "It's not too often you see a real love match. The way that sheriff defended you told me he was a man proud to stand by his woman."

Lydia swallowed hard, remembering how Wesley had defended her. He definitely hadn't shown any distrust in her then. But what about all the other times?

"I know I'm the last person to be offering advice on this, but don't let your pride blind you. Take it from me. It's a hard life to live, Dr. Muir."

Lydia inhaled sharply at his last words. The familiar smells of formaldehyde and putrefaction fumes that filled her lab barely fazed her over the pleasing sound echoing in her ears. "You just called me Dr. Muir."

Dr. Webber smiled, which was a first, as well. He scratched the side of his white-haired head and pushed up his glasses on his nose. "Well, I suppose it would be disrespectful of me to call the director of forensic anthropology anything but her earned title, don't you think?"

Her mouth dropped. "Are you serious? I got the job?" Or was this some kind of cruel joke? She braced herself just in case.

"Let's just say, I've been watching you. I think you're quite capable for a supervisor position, especially after this case. You've proven you'll go deeper to find the truth. Maybe even too deep." He chuckled.

"Yes, I will. I take my responsibilities very seriously."

"Just remember, sometimes it can be quite dangerous to know too much. There are people who will try to stop you from drudging up the truth. I want you to be careful. I would hate to see you get hurt...or worse."

This man was so full of surprises today. "I have a feeling, Dr. Webber, that you care more about me than you let on."

He cackled. "You and your feelings, Dr. Muir. But I guess they've never let you down before?"

"Never."

"All right, then, the job is yours, and that

includes my lab and my office, but if you don't mind I'll start the packing tomorrow. I'd like to play a little hooky today. I have some personal things I need to attend to."

"You? Hooky?"

He wiggled his bushy eyebrows and tossed her the keys to his office and all the offices in the department. "Lock up when you're finished here."

Lydia watched her predecessor exit the room. When the door closed shut, she prayed silently, *Thank You, Jesus, for giving me my heart's desire. This job.*

But instead of diving back into her work with gumption, she reached for the phone. An image of the person she wanted to call flashed in her mind's eye.

Wesley.

She felt herself beam, and a sudden burst of excitement at calling him zipped through her. She halted her fingers on the number pad when she realized her heart felt more alive about making this phone call than it did about the promotion.

But that wasn't right. Her heart's desire was her career. Wasn't it?

She put the phone down. Of course it was. This was what she'd worked toward her whole life.

Lydia put her attention into the cadaver on her table. She'd been given a huge honor. God blessed her with the directorship position. This is what she prayed for. The place God led her to as her guide.

So then why the discontent? Where was the peace she should be feeling?

"You and your feelings, Dr. Muir." Dr. Webber's words came back to her. *"I guess they've never let you down before."*

"No," she answered aloud. "They haven't. Only when I've taken my eyes off God." She dropped her scalpel to the table. It clinked twice on the metal top. "Is that what I've done?"

Shame gripped her as she realized the exact moment she'd stepped away from God.

Wesley asked for forgiveness, and what did she do?

Withheld it. Totally not what God would

have her do. She could have shown him mercy. She could have shown him love.

"Oh, Wesley, what have I done?" She ripped her gloves off, blindly tossing them to take her lab coat off.

I'm sorry, God, for missing my chance to show him Your love and mercy. Be with me now. Take the lead again.

She knew her path started at the courthouse. She hoped Wesley was still there. She hoped he would offer her forgiveness, even though she withheld it from him. Did she dare hope for his love, too?

As she turned to her locker to throw her coat inside, her lab door opened behind her. Had Dr. Webber forgotten something? It was just as well that he came back. She wouldn't be taking the job now. Stepping Stones would be her home soon. The islanders meant so much to Wesley. They were his loved ones, and they would be hers, too. No job was worth coming between loved ones. Just like her father said.

God's peace came rushing in. Now Lydia knew she was back on the right path and making the right choices of what God would want her to do. "I'm glad you came back, Dr. Webber. I need to talk to you." She faced him with a smile…that slid right off her face.

"Why do you keep looking over your shoulder?" Wesley asked Calvin.

A bench in the courthouse hall was their seat while they waited their turn to see the judge. Every time a person walked by, Carmichael shrunk back.

"Why am I getting the feeling you don't believe you're safe? What are you so afraid of?"

A man in a classy, fitted suit stepped up close to them. He lingered nonchalantly for a few extra seconds before moving on. Nothing was said, but after the man dispersed, Calvin mumbled, "I'm a dead man. No jail cell will be safe. No country will be far enough."

"Then you might as well start talking, because I'm the only friend you've got."

On barely a whisper, Carmichael leaned in and said, "I didn't kill Jennifer."

"I don't believe you."

"I tried to persuade her to give up the

ruby. That's all she had to do. But she had this crazy idea that we could take it for ourselves and disappear. That we could change our names and finally be free of this business of smuggling that I'd gotten us into. I couldn't believe it when she went through with the theft. I told her to get away as fast as she could, hide out somewhere until I could come for her."

"Hide out? She came to Stepping Stones to *hide?*" Wesley was surprised to not feel a speck of anger about this fact. In fact, he felt himself smirk at the freeing feeling.

"But the island wasn't far enough. When I learned he'd found her, I called her right away to tell her I was coming to get her. But so was he. I managed to persuade him to go with me to get her. I assured him that she would give him the ruby and everything would be fine." Calvin covered his mouth, his eyes wide with the horror only he could see. "I never thought she would swallow it. And in my shock, I didn't see his knife until it was too late. After I saw what he did to her, I knew he would own me forever. I can't ever get away because he's always watching."

Always watching.

Carmichael's words unnerved Wesley for some reason, but he shoved the feeling aside for the investigation. "So you say you were there the night she died, but you didn't kill her? Why did you leave the body?"

"That frizzy redhead showed up right after. I was told to get the ruby, but when she showed up, I hid under the dock to wait for the woman to leave. I figured she'd go and call the police, but instead she dragged the body to a boat and sped off. After no missing-person report was filed and no one reported a body found, I had to come up with another way to compensate for the loss of the ruby."

"The life insurance policy," Wesley surmised. "You faked her death in the Mediterranean so you could put in a claim."

"But it wasn't enough. It'll never be enough. He wants that ruby. He doesn't like to lose money, or anything for that matter. You may think you've got your guy, but this isn't over. He won't stop until he gets that gem. Trust me, my life has been ruined over this, and he will ruin others' lives before he's done. As he says, 'I'm always watching.'"

"I'm always watching. I'm always watching."

"O'Connor," Wesley said, remembering Brian O'Connor's words to him at the gala.

"Yes, you'd think he'd go after emeralds, but he likes his rubies, or at least the banned ones. The U.S. embargo doesn't stop him. Especially when he's got me smuggling for him. Or had. Now he'll really be after that ruby."

"Lydia," Wesley whispered. "She has it now."

"I give her less than twenty-four hours, if that."

Wesley jumped to his feet. "Owen!" Wesley shouted down the hall to his deputy. "Lock him up. No one goes near him. And I mean no one."

"Where you going?"

"To find Lydia." Wesley sped down the hall to the double exit doors. He burst through and took the stone steps three at a time. The medical examiner's building was three blocks away. Wesley prayed at a pace that matched his harried footwork.

Father, You are my guide. Make my path straight and sure to Lydia. Keep her safe and protected until I can get to her.

Wesley jumped the curve and hung a right when he saw the sign in the front of the M.E.'s building up ahead. He rushed into the street to cross and nearly lost his foot under a truck's tire. Horns blared, but nothing would slow him down.

The glass doors to the building reflected the trees and other buildings and his panicked face as he ran up to them and pulled.

Locked.

He shook the handles violently before cupping his hands to peer inside. He banged on the glass and looked again. An unmanned security desk stood against the far wall. Wesley banged a few more times before a guard finally showed up.

Wesley whipped out his wallet to flash his badge. "Open this now!"

The guard fumbled with the lock on the

door. As soon as it clicked, Wesley pulled it wide and yelled, "Where's Anthropology?"

"Fourth floor down the hall. What's going on?"

"Call the police. Tell them possible homicide in progress. Now!"

Wesley took the elevator to the fourth floor, withdrawing his gun before the doors opened onto a quiet hallway.

His breaths came fast as he tuned his hearing for any sounds behind the row of doors. Name plaques of doctors and personnel adorned each one, and when Wesley came to Lydia's he stepped up to the door in silence. No sounds came from the room, or any room. Maybe he'd reached her in time.

Or he was too late.

A clang of something metal hitting the floor inside. Someone was in there.

Wesley turned the doorknob without a click and peered in with the door ajar. Putrid smells hit his nose, and he nearly backed away before he heard someone yell out, "The skull's on the table. Take it!"

It was Lydia, but her voice sounded muffled

as though something obstructed her words. It was too clear to be a gag over her mouth. More as though she was inside something. Wesley pushed the door a little more and spotted the back of O'Connor pulling on the handle of a large metal locker.

Bingo.

Her thought to hide herself made him proud, but he knew that would only get her so far. The way O'Connor yanked on the flimsy handle said she wouldn't be inside for long.

"That's not going to work, Dr. Muir. You see, I can't leave any evidence behind. And that includes witnesses. I never leave witnesses behind, no matter who they are."

"You're not going to get away with this." Her voice sounded venomous.

"I already have. Carmichael will go down for killing his daughter. I left his yacht in Stepping Stones for a reason, you know. Once I have the ruby in my possession, no one will ever know I have it."

"You set the bomb on the yacht? You nearly killed us!"

"And I'm going to kill you still. Although

the headlines will say Anthropologist Makes Off with the Evidence."

Lightning quick, O'Connor snapped the handle off and reached a hand in, pulling her out by her neck. Seeing Lydia's feet lifted off the ground by the man's deft stranglehold, and hearing the gurgling sounds coming from her obstructed throat, Wesley rocketed into motion.

"Let her go!" He aimed his gun toward O'Connor's head.

The man swung around, but in the same moment, brought Lydia to his front. He'd released her throat, but only to use her as a shield. His free arm shot out at the metal table and snatched up something small that fit in the palm of his hand. He brought it to her neck.

Lydia's sharp, painful inhale cut Wesley deep, but he dared not remove his trained eye from the man behind her...and whatever was in his hand.

"Let her go, or I'll shoot."

O'Connor laughed. "This really is working out better than I could have planned. Now the headlines will say Two Corrupt Lovers Escape with the Jewel."

O'Connor adjusted his hand. In his movement, he revealed a flash of something small and silver.

On a rush, Wesley realized the object O'Connor had grabbed off the table was a scalpel. Probably the scalpel Lydia had been using on the corpse lying on the table.

And now her own tools would be used on her...unless he could stop it.

Wesley squeezed his Glock, wanting nothing more than to sink the bullet in O'Connor's head for what he was doing to the woman he loved. "If you kill her, I promise you I will shoot you, but *not* to kill. I will make sure you rot in the filthiest of prisons. There'll be no country-club reformatory for you. I will guarantee it."

"You won't shoot me. It might cause me to slip."

Lydia grew wide-eyed, imploring him to shoot. He shook his head no. He couldn't take the chance that the shot would cause O'Connor to sink the scalpel in.

He looked away from her to avoid her pleading look. From this angle, he caught sight of two uniformed police officers sneaking in a back entrance to the lab. Help had arrived.

Wesley kept his face blank to keep their presence unknown.

"This is your last chance, O'Connor. Let her go."

Lydia's eyes grew wild and kept deflecting to her right. She was trying to tell him something. But what? To shoot?

Yes. But not Brian.

Then who? The only other person was the...*corpse.*

Wesley whipped the gun to his left and filled the dead guy with three additional bullets postmortem. The body jumped with each hit.

And so did O'Connor.

As Lydia expected, Brian twisted around in surprise to see who Wesley shot. O'Connor's hold loosened enough for Lydia to escape his grasp and flee. Wesley rushed forward to grab O'Connor's wrist. He squeezed and twisted it up behind his back until the sharp tool in his hand clinked to the floor.

The two uniformed officers plunged in to handcuff O'Connor and escorted the roaring madman from the room.

Wesley whipped around to locate Lydia only to have her rush into his arms, nearly toppling him over. He plowed his face into her hair and the side of her neck. He pressed into her with tight arms, never wanting to let her go.

But he had to. She was not his to hold so intimately. So lovingly. So completely. With one last inhale to remember her forever, Wesley released her and stepped back.

Only to have her fling herself back into his arms to plant kisses all over his cheeks and chin. He reached for her face to still her shower of affection. What did this mean? His gaze targeted hers with a silent intensity that demanded an answer.

"I'm so sorry," Lydia whispered. "I was wrong. What I said was all wrong. You should be the one person I spend my life proving my love to. Every day."

"No." Her silky hair that had come loose from her bun dripped from his fingers as he pulled back. "You were right. I never should have doubted you to begin with. You never left me when I needed you most. Not on the yacht. Not in the sea when we crashed. And not when a building was coming down around us. You never left me. But I was too foolish to see it. I have done nothing to deserve your love. Please don't give it to me."

"It's too late. I already have. I love you, and I forgive you. For everything. I'm sorry I withheld my forgiveness when you asked. That was wrong of me." She placed her hand on his chest and scrunched his button-down shirt. It felt almost desperate. "I was not following God when I did that. And I wasn't following Him when I came back here, either. I thought this job was my heart's desire, but it's not. You are. I want to be wherever you are."

Wesley exhaled on a deep emptying breath of disbelief. He stared at her in wonder. "I am?"

She nodded and bit her lower lip, looking so insecure. Did she really think he could ever walk away now? No. He knew without a doubt she was the woman who would bring him good and not harm all the days of his life. He could always trust in her, and he would always do the same for her.

"You honor me, Lydia Muir, with your loving and forgiving heart. I love you so much, and I promise I will do my part and trust in you always."

"I believe you, Wesley." She beamed bright. "I believe you."

"Good, but, Doc, you're not going anywhere. God has guided you to this career, and there is no way I'm coming between Him and His plans for you." Wesley jutted his chin toward the corpse. "Plus, this guy really needs you, and judging by him, I would say the local police could use another officer, too. I just might have to move to the mainland and apply for the job. You up for teaming up with me again on future cases? We could hit the streets and become a dynamic investigation duo."

Lydia's eyes lit up with surprise and then excitement.

"Well, we do make a good team," she said with her little smirk. "We'd make headlines, for sure. I can see it now. Dr. Muir and Detective Grant Save the Day."

"Well, actually, I was thinking something more along the line of Dr. *Grant* and Detective Grant Save the Day."

Lydia grew quiet. The exciting playfulness in her eyes liquefied. Tears pooled up on her lids.

"So? How about it?" Wesley tugged her closer, his fingers running along her forearm. "Would you do me the honor of becoming my wife?"

She squeezed her eyelids shut, then reopened them with a trembling smile. "But what about Stepping Stones?"

"Deputy Matthews will make a great sheriff."

"But they're your family. I can't ask you to pick me over them."

"Pick you? Oh, Lydia, don't you see?" He cupped her smooth cheek. "You picked me."

Tears streamed down her face as she nodded. "I always will."

"So, that's a yes? You'll marry me? You'll become my wife? My partner in every way?"

Lydia sniffed again. Her *yes* came out part laugh, part cry.

Wesley scooped her up to rain kisses down on her soft lips. He tasted her tears mixed with his and basked in how warm and full his heart felt with love overflowing.

And peace. *Thank You, Lord. I feel the peace that can only come from You when I am walking with You. Thank You.*

Wesley pulled back and refilled his lungs to capacity on a deep inhale…and gagged.

"I'm sorry, but I don't understand how you breathe easier in this place. No offense, but your lab stinks like rotting hamburger."

Lydia giggled and wiped her tears. "Not for much longer, because I've been offered the director job. Soon I'll have the lab with better ventilation."

"How? What happened? Oh, Lydia, my love, this is so great! I'm so happy for you. When did you find out? Did you know before you left Stepping Stones?" At her wide eyes, he realized he'd yet to let her get a word in. "Sorry, Doc. Go ahead. Tell me how it happened."

"There's not much to tell. Dr. Webber said he thinks I'm capable of a supervisor position. That's all."

Wesley nodded and smiled gently at this beautiful, humble woman. He filled his arms with her again and kissed her with a feather-light kiss on her sweet-tasting lips. He could really get used to holding her and loved that he had a lifetime to do so.

Wesley released her lips but rested his forehead to hers. "Soon-to-be Dr. Grant, I believe you are the right person for the job, and under the present circumstances, I would have to agree with Dr. Webber's assessment on this case."

Her eyes twinkled. "Can you elaborate on your findings, Sheriff Grant?"

"Why, yes, I can. You see, I have found you to be a noble woman, worth far more than rubies. Believe me when I say, my dear lovely Lydia, I have complete and total confidence in you, and I will do so all the days of my life."

* * * * *

Dear Reader,

Thank you for joining me on Stepping Stones Island. I'm glad you didn't let the skeleton deter you from visiting. It is a wonderful place filled with fun-loving people who really care about each other. For some of you, this might be a return visit to our northern Maine island. We're glad to have you back. For our new visitors, you can read Miriam and Owen's story in *Warning Signs* and learn more about them and the rest of their story.

It's in *Grave Danger,* though, where we don't just dig up a skeleton but also dig up Wesley's past to learn what hardened his heart. The world is filled with people who hurt us, but Wesley had to learn that didn't make everyone untrustworthy. I hope you can agree with me that Wesley did redeem himself in the end when he realized a man who gives his wife his trust gives her the empowerment to bring him good all the days of his life. A woman who knows she is trusted by her husband to make good choices for her family is a force to be reckoned with.

And Lydia was the force Wesley needed to understand this. I think many of us wouldn't have faulted her for turning her back on Wesley. It's easy to make our decisions out of righteousness and what we think is fair for us. But maybe offering forgiveness to someone can have an effect on them that will change them for the better, more than our justified judgment. Just as Christ had mercy on us and we strive to live up to His gift, we, too, can offer others the same gift. The gift of forgiveness has a way of empowering people, just as trust does.

Thank you for reading *Grave Danger*. I love hearing from readers. Please tell me what you thought. You can visit my website, www.KatyLeeBooks.com, or email me at KatyLee@KatyLeeBooks.com. If you don't have internet access, you can write to me c/o Love Inspired Books, 233 Broadway, Suite 1001, New York, NY 10279

Blessings,
Katy Lee

Questions for Discussion

1. What do you think is the theme/premise of *Grave Danger?*

2. In *Grave Danger,* Lydia is a forensic anthropologist. Did you learn anything new about this field that you didn't know before?

3. Sheriff Wesley Grant is an angry man. People have hurt and used him for their own gain, and he has lost his ability to trust. Do you know anyone like this? What is it like to be in their company?

4. For Lydia, it was a constant battle to be in Wesley's company. She was forever defending herself, and sometimes her responses were not merciful and what Jesus would have done. Can you think of a similar situation where you had a chance to show Jesus but instead let your pride or anger or hurt lead?

5. God has given us nine fruits of the Spirit.

Love, joy, peace, patience, kindness, goodness, faithfulness, gentleness and self-control are not only gifts for us, but also gifts for us to give to others. We have nine ways to respond to someone's actions toward us. We can give them anger, or we can give them one of these. Can you think of a time you missed an opportunity to give someone one of the nine gifts?

6. What can you do today to start fresh with that person and bestow one of these awesome, life-changing gifts on them?

7. In *Grave Danger,* the ruby plays a role in identifying the skeleton. How much do you know about trace evidence and its role in helping a forensic team solve a case?

8. I relate the story to the Proverbs 31 woman and the value of a good wife being worth more than rubies. I think that so often women look at this idealistic woman in the Bible and think, how does

she do it? The scripture tells us when it says in verse 11 that her husband trusts her. Trust is a powerful motivator. Why?

9. What did it take for Wesley to realize this?

10. The U.S. embargo for the Southeast Asia rubies continues to remain intact as a means to protect the human rights of the people there, but still the slave trade occurs. How much do you know of their plight? Would you consider praying for these people?

11. What character did you relate to most in this story?

12. What was your favorite scene and why?

13. Lydia is a brilliant scientist, but underneath she still struggles with the pain her "geekiness" has brought her. Do you think her constant attempts to prove her capability is a result of that? What might she really be trying to prove?

14. Proverbs 3:6 tells us to seek God's will in all you do, and He will show you which path to take. The Lord is our guide in life. He goes before us to prepare the way. He stands behind us to protect us. He walks beside us as our friend and champion. What does this mean for your life?